Born in Edinburgh in 1906, **John Innes Mackintosh Stewart** was educated at Oriel College, Oxford, where he was presented with the Matthew Arnold Memorial Prize and named a Bishop Frazer's scholar. After graduation he went to Vienna to study Freudian psychoanalysis for a year.

His first book, an edition of Florio's translation of *Montaigne*, got him a lectureship at the University of Leeds. In later years he taught at the universities of Adelaide, Belfast and Oxford.

Under his pseudonym, Michael Innes, he wrote a highly successful series of mystery stories. His most famous character is John Appleby, who inspired a penchant for donnish detective fiction that lasts to this day. His other well-known character is Honeybath, the painter and rather reluctant detective, who first appeared in *The Mysterious Commission*, in 1975.

Stewart's last novel, *Appleby and the Ospreys*, appeared in 1986. He died aged eighty-eight.

BY THE SAME AUTHOR
ALL PUBLISHED BY HOUSE OF STRATUS

MICHAEL INNES

CARSON'S CONSPIRACY

HOUSE OF
STRATUS

This edition published in 2001 by House of Stratus, an imprint of
House of Stratus Ltd, Thirsk Industrial Park, York Road, Thirsk,
North Yorkshire, YO7 3BX, UK.
Also at: House of Stratus Inc., 2 Neptune Road, Poughkeepsie, NY 12601, USA.

www.houseofstratus.com

Typeset by House of Stratus, printed and bound by Short Run Press Limited.

A catalogue record for this book is available from the British Library
and the Library of Congress.

ISBN 1-84232-726-7

PART ONE

CARL CARSON

1

And now Cynthia was on about her son again: her confounded dream-son. *Their* dream-son. Carl Carson wouldn't have minded so much if his wife had ascribed this tedious invention to an earlier marriage of her own. But to involve *him* in it, to endow him with the fatherhood of a child that simply hadn't happened, was surely a bit much. He'd have rather liked a son. All he'd been landed with was a couple of daughters – who had cost him a packet before getting themselves simultaneously killed in a motor accident. At the funeral he'd totted up what he was going to save as a result. But that had proved to be just one of those queer ways the mind behaves under shock. Before the accident, Carl Carson had been an indifferently honest businessman of a moderately prosperous sort. After it, having made the discovery of the mean and ruthless way the universe works, he had fallen into line with it and never looked back. He was among the least scrupulous men in the city of London.

'What we are so sorry about,' Cynthia artlessly prattled to the guests at her luncheon party, 'is that our son Robin fights rather shy of England. It comes, I think, of all that education at Groton and Harvard. He was quite brilliant, they say, at the wonderful Business Studies, and after graduating he forged straight ahead. So his time isn't really his own. Carl and I run over and see him from time to time at a sweet little place at Key Biscayne. You won't have heard of Key Biscayne.'

'Florida?' the elderly man called Appleby suggested on a politely interrogative note.

'Yes, Florida.' Mrs Carson was clearly launched on something. 'In my earlier years,' she said with a sudden and absurd grandeur, 'my circumstances were such that I saw a great deal of the entire United States. But I have always liked retired and unassuming places, as here at Garford. Key Biscayne is so much nicer than Palm Beach or Boca Grande, don't you think? I adore quiet, quaint places. Sometimes we go to the Grenadines. Mustique – a dear little spot near St Vincent. We have a tiny place there, too. Robin is terribly fond of it.'

'We quite envy you,' Lady Appleby said. This was mere politeness, and offered wholly without irony. One of those well-bred women, Carl Carson told himself, who keep irony for their intimates. Although he hadn't been in the neighbourhood for long, Carson felt he knew a bit about these virtual strangers whom Cynthia had enticed to her board. The wife, he'd heard, came of some petty and antique squirearchical crowd in the next parish. The husband might have been a Civil Servant – the kind that just misses a Permanent Secretaryship, and retires a bit early as a result. Unimportant people. But it was annoying to hear them treated to this romancing about the non-existent Robin, all the same.

And Carson had heard it so often before! He knew that a good many people must have tumbled to the fact that Cynthia was dotty, or at least had dotty spells. It had been another of the universe's meannesses, marrying him to such a person. She was the sort of wife whom, in more sensible times, one had kept locked up in an attic. He indulged occasional fantasies in which Cynthia came to a sudden end at the wheel of her car. But if a number of people would have said of her, 'She seems to me a bit mad', nobody – oddly enough – would have dreamed of saying, 'She even imagines she has a son'. Carson had come to suspect, indeed, that Robin was sometimes regarded as one of the poor woman's anchoring sanities: a sober reality protecting her from afar from going further round the bend. Of course, Carson knew, nobody brooded very much over him and his wife in their private lives. He was himself 'prominent', even perhaps a shade notorious, in his own sphere. But, apart from that, and having neither gift nor apparent desire for intimacy of any sort, the couple were no more than acquaintances of virtually anybody in the land. Lunches here, and dinners there: that was about it. And this affected Carl Carson's manner of coping with the Robin business. On the fairly frequent occasions when (so to speak) the myth directly challenged him he simply went along with it. Unemphatically yet without reservation, he acknowledged his son, confident that nobody would be sufficiently interested in this absentee to pursue inconvenient curiosities.

It was a little different with his wealth, since here people *were* inquisitive. Of course his wealth existed, but it irked him a little that it had to be exhibited to the world through, as it were, a magnifying glass of superficial opulence, as in the appointments of his wife's table, the Rolls-Royce in his garage, the pictures that hung (on a confidential hire-and-insure basis) on his walls. There were, of course, people who knew that on Carl Carson the touch of Midas had been no more than skin-deep; that he thought of pounds and dollars in their hundred thousand, even at times their ten thousand, rather than in their millions. But such people commonly had their own reasons for refraining from suggesting that Carson was not as solid as Threadneedle Street or Fort Knox. And since, at one time or another, he had put a number of them on to a good thing, he even commanded a certain loyalty among them. They would leave money in some Carson concern a shade longer than was prudent. But only a shade, he had sometimes had occasion to reflect. His was a world in which there had to be limits to what one would do for a chum. He had discovered that during years in New York. It had become even more evident when he had returned to settle in London – or rather to settle here in the country and twice a week be delivered from that Rolls into the London train.

'Those Caribbean places must be very jolly,' Humphry Lely said. Lely was some sort of painter whom Cynthia had picked up, and he and his wife were the other guests at the luncheon party. Before sitting down, Carson had shown him a *Peter* Lely hanging in the room, and asked, 'Painter an ancestor of yours, eh?' to which his guest had answered, amiably if incomprehensibly, 'No Dutch blood, I'm afraid. But what about the sitter? One of *your* ancestors?' As the portrait was of an aristocratic Caroline person with the appearance of emerging in some fatigue from a high-class bawdy-house, and as Carl Carson was very evidently what used to be called, rather snobbishly, a 'new man', Carson hadn't quite known whether to be gratified or not. So there had been a slight awkwardness – which was presumably why Lely had now offered this hearty remark about distant places.

Carson became aware that a little scallop of caviare had appeared before him. It probably wasn't quite right, that – not at lunch. One of Cynthia's all too frequent *faux pas*. (He wondered what a *faux pas* was.) Uneasy, he took a consolatory gulp of champagne. Then he wondered about that, too. Perhaps he ought to have said hock. You laid on champagne at garden parties as well as at dinners. But perhaps not at lunch? Not that it mattered a damn. Unimportant people. And he had more urgent things to think about. Soon they might be very urgent indeed.

'I'm sure you must be fearfully busy,' Cynthia was saying to the painter on an admiring note. 'Haven't you been doing a portrait of the Lord Mayor?'

'It depends on what you mean.' Lely was amused. 'Not the Lord Mayor of *London*, you know. Quite obscure mayors have got themselves lorded recently.'

'So they have,' Cynthia said. 'Like bishops,' she added brightly.

This piece of ignorance produced a moment's silence, briskly broken by Mrs Lely. Lely's wife, like Appleby's, seemed to be a socially competent woman.

'Humphry – ' Mrs Lely said, ' – do tell. It was rather amusing.'

'Well, yes – I suppose it was. You see, he was a quite preternaturally red-faced chap…'

'Not like his London colleague, then,' Carson interrupted quickly. 'Daubeney is unusually pale. I was noticing it as I spoke to him the other day.'

'Is that so?' For an instant Lely's glance at his host was of a penetrating order. 'Well, the fellow had to be painted in a scarlet and fur affair like an overgrown winter dressing gown. And there were gongs, trinkets and gewgaws draped all over him. Incidentally, the gongs, etcetera, were brought along to my studio several days running by a functionary in a top hat. He stood by while I did justice to them.'

'How very boring!' Cynthia said. 'But if the sitter himself was *interesting*, I suppose the gewgaws wouldn't matter. If he had *strong* features, marked by *experience*...

This inane and silly talk on his wife's part went on for longer than Carson cared for. Then suddenly – for he was a clever man, with whom pennies dropped quickly – he saw what was cooking, and just why this Lely couple had been asked to lunch. Was he not himself exceptionally interesting? When he studied his own features as he shaved every morning was it not strength and experience that he saw written all over them? And could he prudently reveal, either to Cynthia or anybody else, that the four-figure bill fired at him for a portrait wouldn't be exactly a trifle? So if the woman had taken it into her head to have him painted, there wasn't much that he could do about it. He might, of course – bang off at this very moment – suggest that Lely have a go at *her*. But that wouldn't help. There would simply be two portraits as a result, one on each side of a fireplace, like a couple of china dogs.

Carl Carson saw, he marked with interest, that on this trivial-seeming matter he was of a divided mind. The idea of a portrait – particularly by an up-and-coming man, such as he gathered this Humphry Lely to be – tickled his vanity in a mild way. But somehow, and at the same time, he didn't want to be painted. He was proud of being a somebody, but he had an obscure sense that there was a sort of safety in being a nobody; in not, that was to say, scattering unnecessary memorials of himself here and there. It was a rum feeling, this. But it hitched up with a good deal that lay at present rather heavily on his mind.

And now Cynthia had gone back to the charms of the Caribbean again. He'd read in a book, and tried to pass on to her, that one didn't, if a good conversationalist, recur to a topic that had been on the carpet earlier in the sitting. But at least she hadn't gone back to Robin. There was more than irritation, there was even a lurking hazard, in Robin – chiefly because Cynthia was capable of sudden appeals to her husband to confirm one thing, or amplify another in the recent history of her tedious illusion. Responding to these appeals with an air of casual ease was a tricky matter – at least in any sort of vigilant company. There was always the possibility of appearing a shade uneasy or evasive. And nothing was worse for business – his sort of business – than that. One of the things he had to be (or so he believed) was a monument of all-round integrity. The Caribbean was at least okay here. Mustique was even better, since he did, in fact, possess a small property on the island. It was true that in this area of his wife's chatter shafts of obvious minor lunacy were apt to appear, whereas she was always coherent and persuasive about Robin. But that didn't matter. The chap's wife was a bit loco – so people would fleetingly conclude – and why not? Good luck to her.

'I suppose,' the man called Appleby – Sir John Appleby – said, 'that a good many people retire to those agreeable places nowadays. Plenty of sunshine, and no servant problems. Would you think of it yourself, Carson?'

Carson liked thus being 'Carson' rather than 'Mr Carson' quite early in an acquaintanceship of this sort. It was – as it wasn't among Yanks – the upper-class thing. A reply, nevertheless, required a fraction of a second's thought.

'My dear Appleby,' he said humorously, 'I'm blessed if I could afford it.'

'Oh, Carl darling, what nonsense!'

This loyal interjection on Mrs Carson's part was of most harmless order – whereas she might have said, 'Last night I dreamt that the bailiffs had come', or even (more gnomically), 'Twice clogs, once boots'. And her husband immediately went into what was, in fact, a routine.

'Of course, simple tastes – as you can see ours are – will take one a long way. I remind some of my friends of that when they start moaning about unfilled order books and horrible taxes. Take eighty thousand a year. You couldn't own racehorses on it. But you could send a couple of kids to Eton and such places, and have a bit over to stock your cellar. If the money came to you, that is, in the right way.'

'There, no doubt,' Appleby said, 'is the rub.'

Carson accepted this reflection with a confidential nod. It was possible, he thought, that this fellow Appleby knew his onions. Perhaps he had been high up in the Inland Revenue. If so, it was even conceivable that Carson himself had pulled off a smart one against the chap on some occasion now forever buried in the files. It was an amusing thought, and Carson became expansive.

'Of course,' he said, 'there are plenty of people who go off to those places just as they continue to do to Biarritz and Cap d'Antibes: the vulgar rich, as we used to say, with stacks of money to burn. But if you know your way about, you can manage tiptop style on not all that. Call it that eighty thousand – but merely in dollars, not pounds. And there I'm thinking more or less of a family. On your own, fifty thousand – or even forty-five – would run to pretty well anything you had a fancy for.'

'I must remember that,' Cynthia Carson said, 'when I become a widow.'

This remark, although doubtless gamesome and innocent, occasioned a moment of perceptible constraint. But if Carson himself was vexed, it was because of those eighties and fifties and forty-fives. He was recalling that among the sort of people who were his guests at the moment there existed a senseless disinclination to talk in general society about specific sums of money. Moreover the effect of his little speech hadn't been quite of the modesty he'd intended. So he decided, in effect, to declare the meeting closed.

'Darling,' he said to his wife (for people *did* call their wives that), 'perhaps we should have our coffee on the terrace? And then, since it's such a marvellous afternoon, our guests might care to stroll through the grounds.'

'Yes, indeed.' Lady Appleby said this with a rapid decisiveness which entirely masked her finding her host's phraseology mildly funny.

'Yes, indeed,' Sir John Appleby echoed loyally. He may have been judging that nothing but boredom was going to result from association with these newish and rather unattractive neighbours. But if this was his thought, Appleby was wrong.

'Oh, very well,' Carl Carson said somewhat pettishly to his wife that evening. 'Fix it up as you please. But that little dauber must come here. I won't go traipsing off to a studio.'

'But of course Mr Lely will be only too pleased, I'm sure, dear. Such a chance for him! After that obscure provincial mayor, you know.'

'I suppose that's so.' Although Carson knew perfectly well that it *wasn't* so, this tactful speech had its effect. 'By the way, those Applebys from Dream. What about them? Before they put him out to grass, was the chap some tin-pot mandarin in Whitehall?'

'Whitehall? I don't think so. I don't *think* Scotland Yard is in Whitehall.'

'Scotland Yard?'

'Sir John ran it, dear. He was called the Commissionaire, or something like that.'

'Was he, indeed?' Not for the first time, Carl Carson reflected that the woman wasn't merely mad. She was pretty well an idiot too.

2

Carl Carson, who was so clearly not all that keen on his wife, had no particular fondness for his country either. At least until we reflect, we may judge this ungrateful in him. England had done him pretty well. As with John Bunyan's Mr By-Ends, his great-grandfather was but a waterman, and although his grandfather had risen to the ownership of a wherry, his father, while continuing to follow aquatic pursuits, had achieved his share in the family betterment through some years of loyal service to persons seeing to it that a reasonable number of crates of whisky and gin had fallen off the back of lorries serving London's docks. The devotion thus exhibited by Carl Carson's father had enabled him to put a little by. It hadn't, however, been nearly enough to preserve him from eventually being put by himself, and he had in fact been for some six months in gaol when his son Carl was born.

Although there are plenty of self-made men around, few have in fact made themselves from an initial station so strikingly disadvantageous as this of Carl Carson's. How had he managed it? Anybody asking himself this question (but perhaps nobody ever did) would have reflected that the man was seemingly devoid of any sort of intellectual distinction; was equally lacking in personal charm; and – unlike his dream-son – hadn't even the advantage of having passed through a slap-up Business School. What he did possess was nerve, and a certain reach and boldness of imagination. His path was littered with fallen rivals of whom it might be said that he had simply taken the breath away. And to these endowments there was

11

undoubtedly something in the English social structure that gave abundant scope. Yet of that social structure Carl Carson was far from enamoured. This was because England, as everyone knows, is a terribly class-bound place.

Carson would have told himself that he simply hadn't bothered with the lingoes as he moved up the income brackets. He had learnt to play golf, and could have assessed very accurately the financial standing of the loud-voiced, confident men with the showy cars whom he met in the clubhouses. But he hadn't much listened to them, since they were insignificant people whom he was overtaking and leaving in his glittering wake. The habit of inattention had stuck, so that he was still liable to call a magazine a book, and had quite recently had a similar spot of linguistic trouble over Garford House, the country retreat in which we have been present at his entertaining the Lelys and Applebys. Garford House had some quite ancient bits and pieces, so he had managed to signalise his having acquired it by means of a small illustrated article in a society journal. Having gathered, however, that only rather low-class estate agents apply the word 'home' to houses they are seeking to sell to anyone that comes along, he had taken exception to the appearance, in a caption, of the phrase 'the country home of Mr and Mrs Carl Carson'. Unfortunately, instead of insisting on 'residence', which would have passed muster on a slightly formal note, he had insisted on 'seat'. 'The Berkshire seat,' he had made the thing read, 'of Carl Carson Esquire'. This, being distinctly on the pretentious side, occasioned mild amusement among his associates. In low company (which he still at times frequented in a quiet way) he even had to listen to coarse jokes about stately piles. Small misadventures of this kind could irritate him for days. He even told himself occasionally that he would be quite glad to pack up and quit his stuffy native land for good.

And the business of the portrait was proving curiously unsettling. It was going ahead at what he supposed was a brisk pace, since Humphry Lely came over to Garford almost every day to get on with it. (Probably anxious to get his money, Carson thought.) To see a large white canvas brought into your house, virgin except for certain faint pencillings suggestive of a gigantic piece of graph paper; to submit to a good deal of photography (meaning, surely, that the fellow is going to cheat); and then to watch, day by day, the coming into being of something that is another you, and yet isn't: this can be a disconcerting experience to run into. Carson had been told that artists are often cagey about a work in progress, and don't care for its being stared at. But Lely seemed quite indifferent about this. There the thing was, in a big empty room at the top of the house, and quite often when the painter had gone home Carson went back upstairs and peered at it. He didn't get quite the same effect as when studying (and admiring) himself in the shaving mirror. He even felt he was looking at something it might be wholesome to get away from. He wondered about what were one's rights if a commission of this sort wasn't to one's satisfaction. Could one tell the chap to clear out with it, and decline to pay him tuppence? Probably not. And, anyway, that sort of high-handedness was no longer greatly admired.

Then one evening his wife joined him in studying the portrait, now nearing completion. She looked at it in silence for some time, and when at length she turned to him saw with horror that there were tears in her eyes. How Robin, the crazed woman said, took after his father! The likeness was unmistakable, was it not?

This was perhaps the first occasion upon which Carson was really frightened by Cynthia. A woman subject to that degree of delusion simply wasn't safe. She oughtn't to be trusted with a carving-knife, a knitting-needle, or even a hair-pin. He wondered whether, if he took professional advice and went about it in the right way, he could get her put in a discreetly run private asylum.

But at this time Carson's trepidations were only marginally on any domestic front. In the city there were storm clouds looming, rocks ahead. Although normally not much given to metaphorical expression, he did find himself, in interior monologue, employing these and similar poetical locutions. They gave a kind of hitch up, or vague dignity, to what threatened to be a far from elevated turn in his fortunes. If difficulty turned into disaster, it wouldn't, needless to say, be in any way his own fault. So long as financial and industrial conditions were reasonably 'normal', he was amply buffered against any occasional awkward inquiry into this enterprise or that. But when everybody you met prated of recession or depression or slumps, and hitherto cosy concerns were fussing about their cash-flow, and others actually folding all over the place, there was far too much peering and prying going on in banking and accounting and even legal circles. It wasn't in the least, of course, that he expected to be cast into gaol next week. Mountains of confused and conflicting documentation would have to be sifted before anything of that kind could be on the carpet. Still, it would perhaps be only prudent to take time by the forelock now. The wise man strikes while the iron is hot.

These thoughts, which had less of the pitch of poetry than of that proverbial wisdom of the folk available to the long-deceased waterman and his lorry-liberating son, were much in Carl Carson's mind when he was visited at Garford, promptly upon summons, by a useful and spirited young henchman called Pluckworthy.

'You know, I rather like this place,' Peter Pluckworthy said. He had been admitted to what Carson called his library, and was comfortably settled in a large chair. 'It seems my great-grandfather Hubert had very much the same sort of outfit. Long before my time, of course. He had to sell it because he drank so much champagne out of the slippers of actresses. Odd addiction – at least when carried to that excess. If you have to sell up Garford, Carl, it won't be for quite that sort of reason.'

'I'm determined to get a damned good price for it.'

'Hold hard!' Pluckworthy sat up in alarm. 'You're not really thinking of anything of the sort, are you? Why, you've been here no time at all.'

'Things are pretty bad, Peter my boy. Isn't that what you've come to tell me?'

'Perhaps so. Or, rather, quite decidedly. And there's just precisely one thing you must *not* do. Be seen to be drawing in your horns. Carson Universal Credit would be down the drain within a week. And all the other concerns would follow – like the bloody rats of Hamelin town in Brunswick.'

'Brunswick?' Carl Carson was perplexed.

'Where the river Weser, deep and wide, washes its walls on the southern side.'

'Oh, poetry! Still spouting it, are you?' Carson had relaxed. He quite liked the young man. This was partly because of the rather anomalous kind of hey-you condition (by no means ill-paid) to which he had reduced him. Pluckworthy was, in effect, his creature, licensed to move here and there among the Carson enterprises and report on the understrappers as he thought fit. Carson – oddly, perhaps – also liked Pluckworthy because of his old school tie. Not that the lad wore the thing; it was just that you knew at once that he had it in a drawer. But the chief reason for his regard was his discerning in Peter a man who would come clean in a crisis. Or dirty. No nonsense about not touching pitch. If anything, Peter had an instinctive wish for things to grow ever shadier around him. You might put it that he had a fund of recklessness that he'd be only too delighted to draw on. It hadn't been an asset, so far. Once or twice, it had been almost a threat. But it made him a useful man to hold *en disponibilité*. Or, in Carson's own idiom, to have in the bag.

'How's the missis?' Pluckworthy asked. Setting store by the independence he didn't really possess, he took care to come to business, or veer away from it, as he pleased.

'So-so. Imagines things a bit.' Carson glanced warily at his assistant. 'Trivial things, of course. And takes fancies for this and that. She has insisted on my having my portrait painted, for example. It's going ahead upstairs most days of the week. Fellow called Lely.'

'How very amusing! What's he going after: a likeness – or a board-room icon?'

'You talk a great deal of rubbish, Peter.' Carson frequently said this when he hadn't caught on to something, and the conception of a boardroom icon eluded him. 'Tell me about those people in Birmingham.'

So they talked shop, and as they did so Carson's uneasiness grew. He saw connections and implications, for one thing, that had eluded the young man, sharp as he was. He even came to doubt his persuasion that the worst could happen only after that slow scrutiny by cautious accountants and their kind of balance sheets and prospectuses and tax returns and what-have-you. Weren't we living, he asked himself, in a stagnant economy in which reasonable business enterprise was not only discouraged but positively persecuted? It wasn't even as if he was hearing faint footsteps advancing from afar – implacably, perhaps, but at a pace affording opportunity for evasive action. It might be a knock on the door in the small hours the night after next.

Eventually Pluckworthy rose to go, but as he did so Carson's wife came into the room. Cynthia Carson liked Carl's young assistant. She never mentioned his name to anybody without adding the thought that he was so very much the gentleman. This irked Carson. He didn't care a damn whether a fellow was what they called a gentleman or not, but he felt that in Cynthia's reiterated assertion there lurked the implication that most of the people who bobbed up on them did so straight from the gutter. And this was patently untrue. For instance, Cynthia could have made just the same remark about the young dauber, Lely, paint-pots and all. And, no time ago, hadn't there been those Applebys, who had come to lunch in a perfectly friendly if slightly non-committal way? There was a confused strain of feeling in Carson here. We have seen that his own mild regard for Peter Pluckworthy proceeded partly from his perception that the boy wasn't the first of the Pluckworthys to wear boots.

'Hallo, Cynthia – how goes?' Although much the Carsons' junior, and clearly a mere hireling or client as well, Pluckworthy used their Christian names in the most casual way. Cynthia accepted this; she would have declared that it made her feel young again. Carson, if he reflected on the matter at all, probably judged that a young chap who had to carry about with him a surname as outlandish as his assistant's would naturally prefer Billys and Betsys all the time.

'Everything goes quite nicely, Peter, thank you. The cows are in milk, and the sheep are in very good fleece.' It was one of Cynthia's odd intermittent persuasions that, having moved into the country, she was much involved with problems of rural economy. 'But I hope you are going to stay to lunch? The painter, Mr Lely, will be coming this afternoon, and you might enjoy meeting him.'

'I'm sure I should. Unfortunately, I have to hurry away.' Pluckworthy was well aware that his employer, having heard what he wanted to hear (or, rather, what he didn't), was disposed to be rid of him. 'But may I have a peep at the portrait before I go? Carl has told me about it, and I'd like to see it.'

'But of course! I think it's going to be terribly good. We'll go straight upstairs now.'

Carson had to acquiesce in this, although he wasn't sure he wanted the portrait to be seen by anybody. But the thing was, after all, manufactured for purposes of display (whether in a board room or elsewhere) and Pluckworthy seemed a reasonable person to try it out on. So he followed upstairs contentedly enough.

'Have you been hearing anything of Robin lately?' he heard Pluckworthy ask.

'Yes, indeed!' Cynthia was delighted by this interest in her family. 'We think he may be intending to visit us quite soon, after all. He seems to be rather keen on the idea of England. We begin to wonder whether there may not be a lady in the case. A romance! He may have met some nice English girl, you know, who was visiting at the Embassy in Washington.'

Quite frequently nowadays Cynthia added to her basic delusion this further delusion of grandeur. It was an additional exacerbation so far as Carson's nervous system went. Groton and Harvard had been bad enough. This further imbecility was really intolerable. Carson took two steps at a time, in order to come abreast of Pluckworthy and give him a sharp glance. He had once or twice suspected that the young man – unlike all the rest of the world, apparently – had penetrated to the fact of Robin Carson's non-existence. But if this was so, the knowledge wasn't betraying him into a glimmer of amusement now. He merely paused in his ascent for a moment to address his employer a shade more abruptly than usual.

'If your son arrives,' he asked, 'what will you do with him? Suggest taking him into one of your concerns?'

'I'll decide that when I see him.'

Carson was rather pleased at contriving this reply, which held a certain ambiguity relevant to the underlying situation. If Pluckworthy *did* know, it could be construed as exhibiting a decent regard for Cynthia's unhappy mental aberration. If Pluckworthy *didn't*, it was sufficiently crisp to suggest that he regarded the young man's question as having been on the impertinent side.

But now they were in the big, low room that Humphry Lely had turned into a studio. It was under the leads, and it was necessary to transfer to the service staircase to reach it. No doubt it had been the abode of housemaids in an earlier time; light and air entered only through a skylight; among its absent luxuries, therefore, was any sort of view. Presumably the skylight stood in for the 'northern exposure' which Carson had heard of as favoured by painters. He didn't much care for it himself. During the hours in which he had 'sat' he would have been grateful for a window, and even for a distant prospect of Cynthia's imaginary sheep and cows. It was a bleak, bare apartment – and the more oppressively so since every faintest film of dust had been rigorously scoured out of it in the interest of the mystery now going forward. Apart from a nondescript swivel chair, which Lely had explained would not form part of the final effect, the only piece of furniture – also imported by the painter – was an excessively opulent object somewhat verbosely called a *Regence* ormolu-mounted ebonised bureau *plat*. This gilded monstrosity Carson was to be supposed to have appropriated as a desk; he was to be seated at it holding a gold stylographic pen; and Lely explained that he would later supply a congruous background out of his own head.

Carl Carson, who was quite shrewd enough to suspect a hinted satirical intention in all this, advanced on Lely's easel without cordiality and removed a cloth.

'There it is,' he said. 'As far as it goes, that's to say.'

'And it goes jolly well,' Pluckworthy exclaimed cheerfully. He was studying the unfinished portrait with proper attention. 'It's going to be you, Carl, right down to the ground.'

'We'll hope so,' Carson said. He didn't, as a matter of fact, know whether he *did* hope so. And, obscurely, he hadn't quite liked his assistant's form of words. 'For it's due to cost a packet,' he added with gloom.

Pluckworthy laughed abruptly – presumably as scorning this paltry consideration.

'But isn't it marvellous?' he asked, turning to Cynthia. 'Take it from me: the whole soul of the man is going to transpire on that canvas.' Then, as if aware that this mocking magniloquence had taken him too far, he quietened down. He looked puzzled. He frowned. 'Do you know?' he said. 'It seems to remind me of somebody. But I can't think who.'

'Of Robin!' Cynthia breathed.

'Well, yes – I expect there's that. But I haven't yet met your son, have I? It must be of somebody else.'

'Of me, it's to be hoped – if we're to get our money's worth.' Carson said this quite crossly. 'The bloody thing's called a portrait, isn't it?'

'Again – well, yes. But surely...' Pluckworthy broke off, and his frown deepened. 'Me!' he said suddenly. 'It reminds me of *me*. Elusively, of course. But the me I see in my own photographs.'

Not unnaturally, this occasioned a moment's silence in the attic. It was Carson's first thought that the young man had produced this sudden and bizarre statement preparatory to making a ludicrous but scandalous claim upon him: declaring, in fact, that he was his employer's bastard son and entitled to cash in upon the fact. For a wild moment, Carson even wondered whether this could conceivably be true. He had no sooner seen that it could not than he came by a less disconcerting but yet faintly disturbing perception. There was a certain validity in what Pluckworthy had said. Between Carson's portrait as it was evolving itself on the canvas and the young man now staring at it a fortuitous resemblance did exist. Pluckworthy might look rather like this when he was turned fifty. Alternatively, Lely's work suggested that Carson might have looked rather like Pluckworthy twenty-five years ago. In addition to which, there was the further corollary – whimsical, indeed – that if Robin Carson had existed he might have been not unlike the young man now gaping at Robin's putative father's portrait.

But the thing was elusive, as Pluckworthy himself had said. There was nothing striking about it. All that it need have suggested was the reflection that Peter Pluckworthy must have had his own photographic image much at his command. Carson, however, found himself otherwise affected. It might have been said of him that – like the boy who springs up from his knees in Robert Browning's poem – he had been stung by the splendour of a sudden thought.

'Perhaps so,' Carson said – casually, but favouring his assistant with a hard look the while. 'However, you needn't go round prating about it. And now, we'll get you a drink, and you'd better be off. But don't, in the next day or two, find yourself too far from your telephone. I'll be contacting you.'

3

Although the thought was from the first indeed a splendid one, it was only gradually, and with a good deal of groping, that the elements of Carson's conspiracy came together in his mind. At first it was hardly a conspiracy at all, since he saw himself as a lone operator, manoeuvring and manipulating other people, but taking nobody into his confidence.

He had been much struck by the sagacity of Pluckworthy's warning about the hazardousness of being detected as drawing in his horns. It went without saying that for what he had begun to contemplate with some urgency he would require a great deal of ready money, or at least of what was the next thing to that in his peculiar world. But if he started liquidating assets in a big way, and with no apparent financial or commercial objective in view, there would soon be plenty of people asking why. Of course he could go to work cautiously, so that eventually adequate funds were free and within his instant grasp. But the more he thought about one probing or another of his affairs that might already be going on, the less leisure did he see for anything of the kind. He had to create a situation, a crisis situation that yet held no hint of his true design, in which his suddenly requiring a great deal of ready money would appear not merely blameless but positively laudable.

Carson possessed, as has been recorded, very considerable resources in the imaginative way. Had he become a scientist, he might well have been one exceptionally fertile in the crucial field of forming hypotheses. As a novelist or playwright, he would not have eschewed extravagant situations and hazardous *tours de force*. Addressing himself to his present problem, and examining its various facets as here outlined, he had found all sorts of promising schemes coming into his head. But when, one by one, he chased them up he invariably came on a serious snag. He thought, for example, of being stricken by some rare disease requiring years of costly treatment somewhere in the Himalayas. That would at least get him out of the country – perhaps uncomfortably on a stretcher, but at least moderately provided for in the way of cash. But in that particular regard moderation was something he didn't care for. Extradition, moreover, was an engine nowadays conceivably operative even amid the snows of Everest. He had to vanish. Be dead to the world. *Dead*. That was the crux of the thought that had fleetingly come to him.

But at what point, if any, would he actually be breaking the law? As his plan began to take shape, Carson asked himself this question with some anxiety. It must not be thought that, as was the case with young Pluckworthy, he found the notion of illegality attractive or exciting in itself. He would have described himself as a law-abiding man – meaning thereby that he had no impulse to go shoplifting or avoid paying for a dog or television licence. There were, of course, more complex fields in which the largest legal luminaries might differ as to the legitimacy of this or that. In those fields one could allow oneself what might be termed a reasonable private judgement and some freedom of manoeuvre.

It wasn't illegal to be dead. It wasn't even illegal to be content to be believed dead, unless some element of fraud were involved. Was he heading towards fraud? He couldn't see it. The money he was going to disappear with was his own – or most of it was his own – and this could not be affected by the manner in which he chose to make it immediately available to himself. It was true that, in a few months' time, various people might be asserting their right to chunks of it. But that would be merely a civil matter, and in any case he wouldn't himself be taking much interest in such claims. The main point was comfortingly clear. Even if something went wrong – even if, so to speak, they yanked him out of his grave – there would be a good deal of head-scratching before they found out what to charge him with.

But nothing was going to go wrong. Nothing *could* go wrong. His plan, although it still had some rough edges he must work on, was simply too *clever* to go wrong. More precisely, its mainspring was to be so simple yet of so shattering an effect as to place it quite beyond the conceiving of any copper or private eye in England. Had it not started up in his mind like a creation – which is the hallmark, he had somewhere read, of genius on a job? Chaps like Einstein, and the earlier one who had been stopped short by the falling of an apple: their minds had worked that way.

But neither of these fellow-geniuses had, so far as he knew, been married to a Cynthia. And Cynthia was one of the rough edges. It was going to be a tremendous shock to Cynthia – and what would be the effect of that? With any luck, of course, it would simply send her further up the pole – so wacky that nobody would listen to her. But what if it had the contrary effect? What if his wife turned wholly *sane*? What if she announced, not on any trick cyclist's couch but to some rozzer, dick or flic, even perhaps to a judge, that Robin was an airy nothing, that she'd never had a son? Undeniably, the fat would then be in the fire, all right. But never mind, he said to himself. Never mind; these things take time; time to be over the hills and far away; *excelsior!*

This last spirited ejaculation framed itself almost audibly on Carson's lips as he climbed to the attic for what proved to be his final session with Humphry Lely. Having never had occasion to peruse the poetry of Longfellow, he was unaware that the scrap of dubious Latinity had once accompanied a stiffer ascent and presaged a distinctly chilly end.

Artist and sitter entered the improvised studio together. Lely removed the cloth from the easel. They stood side by side, looking at the painting.

Just this hadn't happened before. Becoming conscious of the fact, Carson wondered about it. Perhaps there was a convention involved, which he had hitherto obeyed without being aware of it. He had preserved from early days the habit of being on the look out for small social things he hadn't got the hang of. But this thought detained his mind only for a moment. It was the painting itself that he continued to feel uneasy about. There wasn't much sense in that. It had, of course, been idle chat about the painting which had triggered off the great thought. But there was nothing at all important about that; nothing about Lely's daub was anywhere near the centre of his design; his sense of discomfort before the thing lay in some other area.

'Just what would you say you're up to?' Carson was startled to hear himself ask an almost philosophical question, which wasn't his style at all. But he persisted with it. 'I mean to say, just what do you aim at?'

'Bread and cheese. Shoes for the kids.'

'There's going to be that, I suppose. And fillet steak for quite some time as well.' Carson had to make an effort to capture this lightness of air. 'But it's not what I mean, Lely. A young fellow of mine, looking at the thing lately, asked if you were going after an icon. It seems an icon is something you find in Russian churches, and lurking in Russian homes and hovels. So it didn't make sense.'

'I'm not so sure about that. When a painter made that sort of icon – probably of the Blessed Virgin – he was out to produce something evoking reverence. And there's always been plenty of that all over the place. Think of a Rigaud of Louis Quatorze.' Lely paused, but Carson, being unable to achieve this think, remained silent. 'Plenty of it in this country, too,' Lely went on. 'Both in pigment and marble. Newton with his prism and silent face. Or Watts doing Tennyson or Browning. Icons, decidedly.'

'You're not after *that*,' Carson said, getting his bearings at last.

'Well, no. Then there's the likeness. There must have been a time when the ability to get a likeness out of some blobs of paint on a palette seemed downright miraculous. Most of the affairs you see at the Academy every year are likenesses – or likenesses cosmeticized. Over the past hundred years or so, the likeness has been taking some hard knocks from the photograph. On Tennyson, for instance, Watts and Julia Margaret Cameron were already neck and neck. Well, that leaves the portrait. By and large, the thing we're now looking at aims to be a portrait.'

'The portrait adds something to the likeness?' Carson, so little a fool, was now right on the ball. 'It's more informative?'

'So they assert.' Lely was cautious. 'But, you know, a lot of nonsense is talked about it all. Shakespeare was sceptical, wouldn't you say? There's no art to find the mind's construction in the face. One may smile, and smile, and be a villain. It's only the real swells that manage it. Raphael, painting a pope. Or Rembrandt, late on.'

Carson was able to reflect that the chance of Humphry Lely being a Raphael or Rembrandt was insubstantial. He continued to be uncomfortable, nevertheless. And something of this Lely perhaps discerned, and was thereby prompted to his next remark.

'But it seems to me there continue to be vestigial magic associations surrounding the whole thing. Have you noticed there are people who hate even being included in a snapshot? They slope off on any excuse that comes into their head. And in primitive societies it can be very marked – or even in some not so primitive. Arabs, now. They invented mathematics, and heaven knows what. But aim a camera at one, and he'll knock it out of your hand. Probably give you a bloody nose as well. And it isn't our sort of western nonsense about the invasion of privacy – although that may have the same roots, I suppose. It's a superstitious belief that if I possess your likeness I thereby hold some supernatural power over you. Every established portrait painter has had soldiers and sailors, debs and duchesses, in whom the same sense has detectably lurked as they sat. Do you mind if we now get on?' It seemed to be the implication of this question that Carson was himself not immune from the irrational responses that Lely had so fluently discussed. 'It's just that left ear, you know. I seem to have failed to hollow my way into it.'

So the ear was attended to at some length – and a good deal to Carson's annoyance. Since he was being depicted sitting at his preposterous desk, and only very slightly in profile, it didn't seem to him that his left ear would have much prominence anyway.

25

Moreover, one ear is surely much like another, and he felt that Lely could have achieved this particular finicky job with the help of an ear belonging to somebody whose time was less valuable than his own. Some kind of apprentice could surely, as it were, lend an ear. Moreover, when the ear was despatched, Lely began fiddling and fussing elsewhere. It was plain from his movements that he was now trafficking in mere minute dabs and dashes all over the canvas. Carson, who didn't know that this particular phase in the creating of a painting is the most joyous and relaxed part of the job, became increasingly impatient. Lely was behaving like a barber in that sort of middling-grand shop in which it is pretended that the customer is excessively fastidious and demanding, and that he has a chauffeur driven car waiting for him patiently outside. Carson had to restrain himself from telling Lely to hurry up and have done with it. You might say that to a hairdresser or even a dentist, but to an artist it would imply a certain lack of *savoir faire*. In addition to which Lely was continuing to chat freely, which hitherto hadn't been his habit while actually at work.

'Fewer and fewer uses for the painter nowadays,' he said. 'It seems incredible that, in the eighteenth century, boys at sufficiently grand schools would commission leaving portraits of themselves by eminent artists, and dump them on the headmaster as they climbed into the family coach. Or think of the Kit-Cat Club: Kneller painting almost every one of his fellow-members just to fit into some panelling somewhere. Kit-cat size, you know. And think, before that, of monarchs sending ambassadors scurrying all over Europe with generously conceived portraits of marriageable daughters. Or Byron commissioning miniatures of himself by the gross, to leave tactfully on the mantelpiece as he said goodnight to lady friends. But when new uses turn up in our great democratic societies the photographer cashes in. Passports, for example. You can't go anywhere today without your mug on one of those.'

'I rather doubt that,' Carson said.

'Again, I never heard of a portrait being cited as evidence of identification in a criminal case. But I remember reading about what you might call a near miss there. Some royalist nobleman cornered during the Civil Wars, and disguising himself as one of his own gardeners in order to get away. He was nobbled and interrogated in his own hall – with his portrait by – I think – the elder Faithorne hanging on the wall directly behind him. But none of Cromwell's chaps raised their heads, so he got away with it. Probably a mere yarn. But quite a good one, don't you think?'

Carson agreed that it was a good yarn, but somehow he didn't care for it. He even wondered whether it was Lely who had made it up.

'And that's the job,' Lely said cheerfully, laying down palette and maulstick. 'Of course I have to take it away – just for a lick of varnish and one or two dirty tricks to get a small wrinkle out of the canvas. My wife's bringing her little van over for it, and she may be here now. You'll have the thing back, however, at the beginning of the week.'

'That's capital – and I'll have your cheque waiting.' Carson said this in a handsome manner, as if something quite unusual and even prodigal were in question. 'And if Mrs Lely is here, we'd better go downstairs now.'

They descended the service staircase in silence. Carson was wondering whatever to do with Lely's damned painting. Perhaps he could present it to the National Portrait Gallery. The place would be bound to accept it with thanks, he supposed, but would then dump it in a cellar so that it would never be seen again.

It was during a pause on a landing that Carson saw that his whole attitude of obscure anxiety in front of this trifling piece of nonsense was absurd. But not merely that. He was in danger, not perhaps of losing his nerve, but at least of feeling it to be a little shaken. Those storm clouds were gathering; those rocks were now dead ahead. He had been delaying too long.

'I think,' he said suddenly, 'my son Robin was mentioned when you and your wife lunched with us?'

'Yes, indeed.' Lely was slightly surprised. 'Mrs Carson said something about him.'

'Cynthia is very fond of him, naturally. She'll be delighted by the news.'

27

'You've had news?'

'Yes – although don't mention it. I'm saving it up as a treat. Robin's coming on a visit in no time. I had a cable from him the other day.'

It was thus that Carl Carson crossed his Rubicon.

4

But affording Cynthia her treat wasn't going to be plain sailing. And would it really *be* a treat? It had for long been his habit simply to acquiesce in her delusion, but he had never before taken any initiative in, as it were, fleshing it out. What would be the result now? Carson had no use for psychiatrists and their like, and his wife's imaginings, although inconvenient and, of course, distressing, had never prompted him to seek any professional opinion on her. He had frequently told himself that there would be time enough for anything so embarrassing and expensive if and when the thing really got out of hand. That had never quite happened so far, and he had gone along with the nonsense without thinking all that about it.

But he had to do some thinking now. There must, he supposed, be a corner of her mind in which Cynthia knew that she had invented Robin; that he had sprung, so to speak, not from her womb but from her head. Might not the news that such a phantasm was about to arrive at Garford simply terrify her to the point of screaming? And if he didn't arrive (as, of course, he couldn't) and she had to conclude that he had met with very considerable misadventure on the way, mightn't she react more badly still – even to that dread point of proclaiming to the world that Robin Carson was a fake? Carson wasn't yet altogether clear about the misadventure; his plan was proving, after all, to be still at an elementary stage; but he knew that misadventure there would have to be. And *speedy* misadventure. A glimpse or two of Robin was something somebody could perhaps be persuaded he had had. But what was going to happen must happen within, say, an hour of the phantasm's touching down at Heathrow.

He did some hard and, of course, knowledgeable thinking about airports. There was the girl who took your ticket and processed it. There was the man who glanced at your passport and nodded you on. There was somebody further – man or girl – who took your ticket again, gave you a second ticket of sorts, and allotted you your seat. And at that you were on board. You had possibly been frisked. You had certainly passed through a contraption which behaved dramatically if you were harbouring large chunks of metal about your person. But that was the whole thing.

In flight there might be some routine stuff about currency or the like, but that was neither here nor there. And at the other end you just got off, went through a passport business – again on the nod unless you looked like some species of dubious alien – and that was it. Baggage collecting and customs people, of course – but they were nothing to worry about. Except, perhaps, for mere tin-pot journeys, there was somewhere, no doubt, a record preserved of the people who had checked in: there had to be, since occasionally whole plane-loads of travellers got themselves burnt to cinders. *But on no normal occasion did your passport and your ticket come simultaneously under the same eye.* So on your ticket you could be Mr Black, and on your passport Mr Brown. There might, of course, be exceptional circumstances, and even certain routes, upon which not all of this convenient state of affairs obtained. You would have to make sure. But, by and large, it held. Provided that Mr Brown had his authentic passport – and visas, if required – he could, if he had a fancy for it, actually travel as one of the Incas of Peru.

It was only very briefly that Carl Carson had to wonder why he had been reviewing these familiar facts. They had never been of any concern to him before, since his own aerial occasions had invariably been as blameless as yours or mine. He realized that they were in his head now simply because his plan was after all less nebulous, was further advanced, than he had been consciously aware of. The time for action had, in fact, arrived.

Carson's thought-processes so far, although tentative in parts and not entirely lucid, were rational enough. This was unsurprising, since cool – even cold – calculation was habitual with him. Quite soon, however, he was to become intermittently aware that a change was taking place. He became wary in areas in which wariness was so superfluous as to be a waste of nervous energy.

The Punters were a case in point. On moving into Garford, the Carsons had for some time made do with domestic service of a rather scrappy sort. There was a gardener, Lockett, with a cottage in the 'grounds', who stuck to gardening and refused to do anything else. A couple of women 'came in' from the village on alternate weekdays and messed around. A third and elderly woman, of somewhat less humble status as having retired from an obscure catering enterprise, also appeared regularly and cooked a dinner. Carson drove his own car. Although it was so grand a car, its owner felt that he was still on the wrong side of a great divide as long as he himself thus sat at its wheel – in addition to which he had to be irritatingly cautious when driving home after well-lubricated business occasions. So he had decided that, in addition to the two non-resident rustic drudges, it would be reasonable and proper to run to a married couple of the superior and professional, but nevertheless all-purpose sort. The Punters, contacted through the advertisement columns of a top newspaper, were the result.

It had turned out, of course, that such couples cost the moon. Carson had been quite shocked by the figures he had seen quoted as necessary to secure their services. They were in a bracket even higher than that of nannies prepared to look after nice children in Jeddah or New York. But the Punters, in addition to having turned up at once, had been surprisingly moderate – although still not exactly unassuming – in their financial demands. Punter himself proved to be every inch, and undeviatingly, a butler; one felt he could have sustained the part with distinction even in a superior West End comedy; but at the same time he was quite willing to assume a peaked cap and drive the Rolls – a function a little outside that of butlers in the traditional hierarchies of English society. Mrs Punter addressed

Cynthia as 'madam' on all available occasions, and seemed only to be waiting with some confidence for the day on which this would become 'm'lady'. Carson's satisfaction with the Punters ought to have been unflawed.

He had nevertheless come to distrust them – and this in a direction that was distinctly odd. Had he taken it into his head that they constituted the avant-garde of a gang of professional burglars, covertly engaged in taking impressions of latch-keys and expertly examining the signatures on oil-paintings and the authenticating marks on the under-side of porcelain figurines, he would have been succumbing merely to the normal anxieties of a man of property. But it was another system of suspicions that Carson had found gaining on him.

The under-side he had one day himself given way to looking at was that of his telephone. Of this particular telephone he was rather proud. It didn't trail a flex. (In this it was probably like the red one habitually toted round by the President of the United States.) He could carry it, or it could be brought to him, anywhere in the house, or even within the nearer reaches of the garden, and put into operation straight away. It was this harmless toy that, being one day alone in the house, he had found himself inverting and studying with care. In other words, there had presented itself to him the dreaded spectre of being bugged. He was suddenly apprehensive that within the sanctity of his own home industrial espionage had reared its ugly head.

He knew that it was silly. He knew that it was in the Far East – in Singapore and Hong Kong and such places – that the anti-bugging people had found a happy hunting-ground of gullible tycoons convinced they were being thus pried into. He even had some money in that sort of thing himself. It was vanity that the anti-bugging crowd preyed upon; it ministered to a man's self-importance to believe that his mere chit-chat was valuable to other people.

The telephone had looked wholly innocent. But that told you nothing. He got a screwdriver and opened the thing up, but of course that wasn't informative either. Then he found he couldn't put the damned contraption together again. He had to pretend he'd dropped it on the marble floor of Garford's hall, and send for a mechanic. It had been a most embarrassing aberration.

And that didn't conclude the matter. Punter could have filled the whole house with the devilish contrivances! His office in the city, too: other villains might have been at work there. Hadn't there been that monstrous affair in the American Embassy in Moscow? And conversations about complex financial manoeuvres were one thing: even substantially caught and transcribed, they mightn't convey much. A simple life-and-death affair (and what better description could there be of what he was taking in hand?) was quite another. The deepest secret could be given away in a sentence.

So the subject was worth going into thoroughly. Carson, although not much of a reading man, read it up. Giving it out that he was thinking of perhaps installing large-scale precautions, he even picked the brains of an expert. What he discovered was interesting and rather startling. Distance wasn't an important factor in the bugging business. Granted adequate instrumentation, you could pick up the conversation of a couple of chattering bedouin across a substantial stretch of the Sahara Desert. But not from amid, say, a populous casbah or a caravanserai. The bug can't filter out din. Conduct your conversation close to a general uproar, or even under a comfortable warm shower, and you are as safe as houses.

There was very seldom, of course, any sort of uproar at Garford. The two village girls (who still came in to do the rough) must have got through their gossiping elsewhere. The woman who cooked had been dismissed, since Mrs Punter cooked very well. Mrs Punter creaked a little, so you sometimes had warning of her approach as a result, much as if she had been the crocodile in *Peter Pan*. As for her husband, he made no sound at all. Of a stiff and almost military bearing from the waist up, from there downwards there was something that seemed immaterial about Punter, so that at times you could swear he was levitating rather than treading the carpet or the parquet. It was hard work conversing with Punter; he had no apparent fondness for saying anything other than 'Thank you, sir', and a particular fondness for saying it when told to go away. Carson suspected that this wasn't quite right in a butler. He had from time to time been in the houses of other men who kept butlers, and had noticed that a little familiar chat between employer and employee seemed to be quite the thing. So he had become, as we have seen, suspicious of Punter, and inclined to wonder whether he was quite what he seemed to be. Carson wasn't prepared to see this suspicion as madness (one mad person in a household being quite enough) but he knew there was a word for it – one of those troublesome para-something words – and that those were particularly liable to it who were occasionally troubled by the fussy and importunate curiosities of other men's accountants and of beastly little lawyers on the make. Nevertheless he did insist on talking to Punter from time to time.

'Punter,' he said, on the day following the completing of the portrait, 'has your mistress said anything to you about preparing Mr Robin's room?' Carson wasn't sure about 'your mistress', although it was certainly what people said in the rather old-fashioned novels he dipped into from time to time. Punter didn't appear put out by it. He had an air of slight surprise, all the same.

'Mr Robin, sir?' Punter asked – and perhaps with eyebrows ever so fractionally raised.

'Yes, damn it – Mr Robin. My son.'

'No, sir. But Mrs Carson would more probably speak to my wife.'

'Well – has she?'

'No, sir.'

'Mr Robin is coming on a visit. From America.'

'Very good, sir.'

This struck Carson as a singularly idiotic thing to say, and for a moment, in the vulgar phrase, he lost his cool.

'Blast it, man!' he said. 'I sometimes can't make you out. Don't you like the job? There's a remedy, if you don't.'

This time, and very understandably, Punter's eyebrows did go right up.

'By no means, sir. And I only trust we give satisfaction. If I may venture on a remark, a household like your own – that of a gentleman of great wealth that is yet conducted in a modest manner – is particularly agreeable to persons like Mrs Punter and myself. On account of our having been, as we always so fortunately have been, only in the best service.'

This speech astonished Carson. It astonished him – so taciturn was Punter's normal habit – merely as being a speech (or 'remark') at all. There was something gratifying in being judged a gentleman of great wealth, which unfortunately wasn't quite his own idea of himself. And 'only in the best service' was gratifying as well. He was in two minds, all the same – uncertain whether to embrace Punter and suggest they have a drink together, or to dismiss him on the spot on the strength of a monstrously impertinent irony. This dubiety (which speaks, after all, for that acuteness of perception which seldom deserted him) held him silent for a moment, so that it was left to Punter to sustain the dialogue.

'Would you yourself, sir, have any instructions to give in view of the young gentleman's imminent arrival?'

'No, no – nothing of the sort. We'll let you know when anything is required.'

'Thank you, sir.'

Punter gave a bow – rather as a prime minister might do at the conclusion of an audience with a monarch – and withdrew.

So the moment for giving Cynthia her treat had come. Affording the first news of Robin's supposed arrival casually to Humphry Lely had been harmless enough, but announcing it to Punter, who, unlike the painter, was permanently on the premises, was different. It would never do if it was one of the Punters who first announced the fallacious fact to Cynthia. Carson had thus, in a sense, jumped his own gun. If he mentioned the imaginary cable, his wife would want to see it. If he didn't, it might be mentioned in her presence on some further casual encounter with Lely. Reflecting on this, Carson roundly cursed the cable. In inventing it he had violated that Law of Parsimony which has become known to logicians as Occam's razor.

Being no logician, Carson didn't actually call it this. He just told himself that one ought to be sparing with one's fibs. This trifling one had unexpectedly proved distinctly awkward. Then he remembered that cables, like inland telegrams when such things still were, frequently arrived by telephone. Perhaps he could get away with that. But there was something ominous about this small difficulty. It suggested that other difficulties, large as well as small, were bound to be on the way. The way was the way to freedom, nevertheless. He must simply drive ahead.

In the event, it didn't go too badly. It went rather well. It went rather too well, indeed, to be quite reassuring. This last feeling in himself Carson would have found it difficult to explain. It was partly a matter of Cynthia's having taken his news so very much in her stride. Of course she had lately been *expecting* Robin to turn up. Her conversation, both with her husband and others, had frequently been turning on the fact. At times it had been distinctly gushing conversation, as if the mere prospect of the event might at any moment induce a transport of excitement. But now she received what her husband had to announce much as if Robin were a regular weekend visitor. She asked no questions, whether about that cable or anything else. She had simply put down her knitting (she had never lost an early habit of knitting socks) and rung a bell.

Except in hotels and places, ringing a bell was an action Carson tended to avoid. He had a vague feeling that it was an archaic practice no longer followed except in classes of society in which it was easy to go wrong. If he wanted Punter, he would stick his head into the man's pantry, or even just give a shout, rather than tug at a rope or push a button. So only Cynthia ever rang a bell, and only Mrs Punter ever answered it. She did so now.

'Mrs Punter, dear,' Cynthia said, 'my son is coming on a visit. We must have a nice room ready for him. Perhaps the one with the big bow window.'

'Yes, madam. The blue room.'

'The blue room?' Cynthia repeated doubtfully. She could never remember that she had a blue room – perhaps because she associated the adjective not with the sky, the sea and the eyes of new-born babes, but with pills, nasty music, improper movies and dismal states of mind. 'But, yes – of course. I'm sure it's not dusty, or anything of that sort. But do remember soap. It can be so awkward without soap. And I'll speak to Lockett about some nice flowers.'

'Very good, madam. Will it be tomorrow that Mr Carson arrives?'

'Mr Carson?' Suddenly Cynthia was at her most completely vague – and then, equally abruptly, decisive. 'Thursday,' she said. 'You will so like dear Robin.'

'Thank you, madam.' And Mrs Punter went away.

Carson had said nothing about Thursday, and he ventured to point this out now.

'Oh, it's sure to be Thursday,' Cynthia said calmly. 'Thursday has been my lucky day ever since the tombola.'

Like so many of his wife's remarks, this one was meaningless to Carson. Perhaps the tombola had been some nonsense at a church fête or Women's Institute jamboree. Cynthia rather liked being a local lady of some consequence at that sort of thing. And the same underlying idea attended her next remark.

'I wonder, Carl, whether Robin has been taking an interest in stock-raising. If so, our shorthorns ought to appeal to him, don't you think?'

Shorthorns weren't quite as mysterious to Carson as were tombolas. Gentlemen farmers, among others, went in for them. But he was no more a gentleman farmer than his wife was a lady one, and the shorthorns were as mythical as Robin himself. The thought came to him to imagine Cynthia in the witness box at any sort of criminal trial. (Not, he told himself parenthetically, that she could legally give evidence against *him*.) The judge would listen to her for five minutes, and then quietly suggest to counsel that she had enlightened the court enough. Although privileged to be his wife, Cynthia was definitely among the unimportant people. If she couldn't be relied on, neither had she to be reckoned with. He could forget about her, and get on with the thing.

Carson picked up the portable telephone, and made an appointment with Peter Pluckworthy.

5

'A cat-nap,' Pluckworthy shouted. 'Why the hell should I take a cat-nap? I don't want a cat-nap. I sleep perfectly well, thank you, at proper times.'

'Kidnap,' Carson shouted back. 'Not cat-nap, you idiot. Kidnap.'

The shouting was because of the traffic thundering by. For this most secret conference Carson had chosen a locale with meticulous care. He had reconnoitred the terrain the day before, and hit upon this kerb-side café where they were now sitting. As not in Paris and certain other continental cities, such ventures in London are commonly newfangled, skimpy, and comprehensively infelicitous. If you want to be deafened by every sort of vehicular outrage, you sit down at one of their nasty little tables. It is without even a newspaper on a stick being provided by the establishment. After some ten or fifteen minutes, you may be brought a cup of tepid coffee.

Carson didn't want coffee, and he didn't want to be deafened. But he did want to avoid the menace of the bugs. And this he was certainly achieving. Not the most refined acoustic device conceivable could have unscrambled a conversation from the din. Raising his voice still higher, he endeavoured to explain this wise precaution to his companion. What Pluckworthy immediately gathered from it was that his employer had gone nearly as dotty as his wife. Madness was infectious, no doubt. Yet it wasn't so much insanity of any recognizable sort as a mere crumbling of nerve. So, even more than commonly, he must mind his p's and q's with Carson. If the man had some outstanding villainy in mind, that might mean something exceptional in the way of bribe or bait for *him*. And be amusing as well. But, first, Carson needed to be recalled to his senses. This lunatic fit of jitters didn't augur well for his reliability in a tight spot.

'See here, Carl,' Pluckworthy said. 'It's nearly one o'clock, and what I need is a decent meal. You're going to give it to me.' He paused for a moment, and then named the most expensive restaurant that came into his head. 'We'll go there.' With this, Pluckworthy jumped to his feet and flagged down a passing taxi. 'Get in,' he commanded briskly.

And, obediently, Carson got in.

The change of setting was a success. Almost with his first glass of wine, Carson relaxed a little. When the bottle was finished, and brandy before them, confidence had fully returned to him. He even managed to see his fears about the bug as having been almost comically excessive. Nevertheless, when he judged the time had come to unfold his plan (or part of it, perhaps it should be said) he was unable to resist leaning confidentially over the table and dropping his voice almost to a whisper. But Pluckworthy, who at least for a space was continuing to control the situation, would have nothing of this.

'Quit it, Carl,' he said, leaning back in his chair. 'If you behave like all the conspirators in Rome, people will really start getting interested in you. Perfect strangers – those two fat men at the table in the window, for instance – will do their best to listen in, just as a matter of idle curiosity. Unwind, and keep it chatty, old boy.'

Carson, although resigned to his underling's use of his Christian name, resented 'old boy' as intolerably familiar. 'Chatty', however, reminded him that the occasion was eminently one on which Pluckworthy had to be chatted up. And, of course, bought, as well. There would be a haggle over the figure later. At the moment, he was relying chiefly on what he judged to be the young man's temperamental liking for a wild-cat scheme.

'Cat-naps,' Pluckworthy said telepathically. 'We'd got as far as cat-naps. Or, rather, we'd advanced from that to kidnaps. Carry on from there.'

'*You're* going to carry on from there, my boy.' Carson had resolved to be spirited. 'You're going to be kidnapped, believe you me. But not as a mere nobody called Peter Pluckworthy…'

'Thank you very much.'

'Just keep your mouth shut for a minute, and listen. You're going to be kidnapped – at or near Heathrow, I think – as my son.'

'Your son? Don't make me laugh.'

'Yes – my son.' Carson, although he reiterated this firmly, was checked for a moment. There came back to him the suspicion that Pluckworthy *knew*. But that was really neither here nor there, since the fact of the non-existence of the person in question could be acquiesced in at once, if need be.

'Robin?' Pluckworthy asked – surely teasingly. 'The one Cynthia sometimes tells me you meet up with at that dear little Mustique?'

'Yes – Robin. As Robin Carson you're going to be kidnapped. Kidnapped and held to ransom. Get?'

'I get.' Pluckworthy's eyes had rounded in a fashion that Carson judged distinctly hopeful. 'The hell of a big ransom, no doubt?'

'Big, but not out of all reason big. Enough to set me up very comfortably elsewhere.'

'Key Biscayne, perhaps? I seem to have heard of it too.'

'Of course not. Somewhere, naturally, that I've never been to before.'

'A new and purer life. But just where is the ransom-money coming from? A guild of philanthropists?'

'The money will be my own, naturally.' Carson couldn't resist a note of modest pride as he said this. 'But, of course, getting it together is the ticklish thing. If word were to get round that I was drastically increasing my liquidity ratio, the fat would be in the fire at once. You do see that?'

'Yes, of course.' Pluckworthy was impatient before this elementary fact. 'If a dubious character like you, Carl, suddenly exhibits a marked liquidity preference, the prison gates pretty well begin to yawn.'

'You can put it that way, if you like.' Carson, naturally, wasn't too pleased by this unseemly expression. 'But everybody knows that ransom-money has to be got together in the most hush-hush way. It has to be managed, for instance, so that the police can say they know nothing of your intention to pay up. So here will be me, going ever so quietly round, moaning "My son, my son!"…'

'Moaning "Pluckworthy, Pluckworthy!", you mean.'

'I've told you to shut your trap, haven't I? Everybody will be tremendously sympathetic, and make no end of necessary transfers and cashing of cheques just as quietly as may be.'

'You have a point there.' Pluckworthy glanced with a certain – and unusual – admiration at his employer. 'But why pick on me to be the victim of this bogus kidnapping? Is it because I talked some nonsense about that portrait being a shade like me – and therefore your son and I having a possible lick of one another?'

'It did cross my mind, Peter, as being conceivably useful. But it's not much of an idea, is it? I pick on you because you're a reliable man.'

'Thank you very much. By the way, there isn't a real Robin Carson, is there?'

'Of course not.' Carson – as he had resolved to do – took this point quite casually. 'But everybody believes there is. It's quite extraordinary. And if you are an exception, it says something for your wits.'

'The plan does say something for yours. The police can't rescue Robin, because Robin doesn't exist.'

'And they can't capture the kidnappers, because they don't exist either.'

At this, Peter Pluckworthy laughed abruptly – and also rather loudly, so that the two fat men at the nearby table turned to stare at him.

'I suppose,' he asked, 'it has to be rather a spectacular kidnap – enough to engage at least a mite of attention by the media?'

'Of course.'

'Has it occurred to you, Carl, that to make the papers with the kidnapping of a non-person by other non-persons will be technically on the demanding side?'

'That's where you and I put our heads together,' Carson said.

6

So it *was* a conspiracy. Carl Carson was well aware that 'conspiracy' was a word much endeared to Attorneys General and Directors of Public Prosecutions. To be a conspirator was held – for some totally irrational reason – to be considerably more heinous than to be a crook on one's own. And, as soon as they began to move in concert, he and Peter Pluckworthy were conspirators.

Or were they? Carson had a great respect for the law. He liked, that is to say, to think of legality in generous and comprehensive terms. As spreading wide, in fact. A man mustn't be too ready to feel himself outside it. Lawyers themselves understood this, and plenty of them were prepared to exercise great powers of mind to make juries believe, and therefore judges declare, that their client's intentions, and even actions, had been as blameless as the skipping of lambs in spring. So although he and Pluckworthy were now undoubtedly cooking up something together, could it really be regarded as a course of conduct insusceptible of some sort of favourable interpretation in the hands of a wily chap in a wig and gown?

Carson spent a little time considering his position in this hopeful light. The money involved was, he reiterated to himself, his own – or at least it would be difficult to prove that any very substantial part of it was not. For his own legitimately private purposes – he heard this admirable barrister explain – Mr Carson had been obliged to make various redispositions which, if they became public, might readily be so misinterpreted as to occasion alarm and despondency among the minor investing classes. This he had been magnanimously prepared to go to considerable trouble to avoid. So, being a man of some imagination and resource, he had evolved a plan, in itself no more than a harmless and amusing prank...

On 'prank', however, he pulled himself up – detecting in the word what scribbling fellows called a hollow ring. You can't fake, any more than you can actually effect, a robustly sensational kidnapping and holding to ransom without prompting a good deal of activity by the police. Extensive police operations in such a field cost money, and – at least in the pious sort of theory that would be advanced – divert the forces of the law from more fruitful activities. If on nothing else, they'd get you on that.

So this whole line of thought was a waste of time, and it would be better to acknowledge the risks and get on with the job. He had merely sketched his rough idea to Pluckworthy at that rather heavy (and wickedly expensive) lunch. No doubt Pluckworthy's own brains – which were by no means to be despised – would now be at work on it. But the main burden of the thing, what might be called the intellectual labour, remained with him. And he had to admit that there was still a good deal of mere groping in front of him. He was rather in the position, he reflected, of some poor devil churning out a whodunit – pushing along, he didn't know quite where. He did, of course, command that beautiful main thought: that for an hour or thereabout Robin Carson would come into existence and then again cease to be. (Henry James himself – of whom Carson hadn't heard – could not have been more overcome by the 'beauty' of an idea than was our hero when confronted by this one.) Of course the imagined Robin would simply have become the quite real Pluckworthy again, and this meant that Pluckworthy would thereafter be something of an inconvenience. He would know far too much. But what he wouldn't know was the destination – some highly agreeable destination, it was to be hoped – for which his late employer had departed.

Would there have to be other inconvenient persons? Cynthia had perhaps to be reckoned as in that category. Knowing her dream-son to have been kidnapped and subsequently killed (for that, Carson quite understood, would have to be the implication) would she not be drastically cured of her delusion, and announce Robin to have been a fiction? He had dimly foreseen this risk already; now it became enhancedly formidable. Of course, it was true here, too, that nothing of the kind could happen until he was over the hills and far away. But it might mean that he would be hunted for. Unless, that was, he had himself joined Robin among the reputedly slain. Of that, also, he had thought already, but so imprecisely that he had almost forgotten about it. And yet it was the crown of the whole thing! Decidedly, he must now hold on to it, fit it in as he could. Wheels within wheels, he told himself rather desperately. The beauty of the idea wasn't exactly going to be the beauty of simplicity, after all.

Kidnappings are usually perpetrated by gangs. On the continent, where they have been chiefly fashionable, the gangs may be suddenly-assembled small armies, sufficiently equipped with automatic weapons to overpower even substantial opposition from security police, private bodyguards and the like. Nothing of the sort was in question for the projected operation. But wouldn't at least two or three accomplices be required? Carson was surprised and displeased to notice the term 'accomplices' coming into his head. 'Assistants' might be better. But, whatever they might be called, where were they to be found? A citizen as blameless as himself naturally had no connections with anything that could be called an underworld. If suddenly required, for instance, to find what was known as a hired gun, he would be as stumped as the local vicar or GP. For a moment, and surprisingly, he found his mind turning to Punter. Perhaps because of the mask-like effect achieved by Punter's perpetual 'Thank you, sir', and the like, he had several times extended his doubts about Punter beyond the bugging business to wondering whether the man might not be the kind of villain that gets along on sudden and ruthless violence; whether, in fact, Punter might not any night tie him up with his own pyjama cord and depart with the spoons.

This was an extravagant apprehension, but it did set Carson wondering whether it mightn't be possible to enlist Punter for the task ahead. Eventually, however, he dismissed this as a messy idea.

And, even as he did so, he remembered that he had already formulated, if only in a hazy way, a much more elegant proposal. Pluckworthy had been on to it with his talk of non-persons. Work it out properly – make it, for example, a nocturnal affair – and no bogus kidnappers need be brought in. The captors *could* be as phantasmal as their supposed captive. Pluckworthy was going to be kidnapped. Let Pluckworthy also do the kidnapping.

A choreographer, supposing Carson to have had so unlikely an acquaintance, might have told him that he was here setting himself a pretty stiff problem in the contriving of a *pas de deux*. But Carson's confidence was growing. What has been called by a poet the fascination of the difficult can – one has to suppose – beset quite other than poetic characters. Those are perhaps particularly vulnerable to it who have, in the old phrase, a good conceit of themselves.

Then, quite suddenly, Cynthia became a problem again. He had got home from a long day in town, and was applying himself rather fretfully to the cocktail cabinet in the drawing-room. It was an elaborate affair, the cocktail cabinet – all chrome and perspex and funny little concealed lights – and he had come to be a shade doubtful about it, and particularly about its location. There were plenty of advertisements – in the colour-supplements and such places – which showed prosperous and persuasively top people standing beside, or in the more elaborate examples even within, this particular prestige possession. But Pluckworthy had recently referred to the Garford one as the 'bar', and made fun of the natty little stools that had come along with it for free. Punter, too, could be detected at times as casting upon it a supercilious eye, as if it had never been his demeaning lot to keep company with such an object in all that long career in the best service which it had been his good fortune to share with his wife. This social dubiety could mar Carson's pleasure in concocting himself even an unassuming Bloody Mary. He was concocting one when Cynthia came into the room.

'Do you know?' she asked. 'You'll never guess!'

'I don't want to. Have a drink.'

'Just the plain tomato juice, dear. Only fancy! I've discovered who it is.'

'Who who is?' Carson moodily poured Cynthia her dismal draught. 'I don't know what you're talking about.'

'That's what I say. You'll *never* guess.'

Carson was, of course, used to this sort of conversation with his wife. It frequently veered into something fairly mad. And that was the way of it now.

'Robin's friend,' Cynthia said.

'Robin's friend?' Carson's heart already foreboded ill as he repeated this. 'Just what do you mean: Robin's friend?'

'The romance, dear. We must be clear-sighted, you know. We must be realistic. Robin will love to be with us again, of course. But the main attraction is Mary Watling.'

'Mary Watling! You're off your…' Carson checked himself. He needn't enunciate the obvious. 'The daughter of those stuck-up people at the Grange?'

'The Watlings aren't stuck-up, dear. Only very well-connected – which will be nice for Robin. Robin is just a *little* fastidious, don't you think?'

'No doubt.' Carson had never heard of Betsey Prig and her final courageous assertion that Mrs Harris existed only in Mrs Gamp's mind. Nor, had he done so, would it any longer be feasible to emulate her now. He was stuck with a real Robin. 'But why should you imagine…'

'Quite a long time ago, Mary had let something slip about Robin. Almost as if there were a secret! This time, she was a little evasive, and it was almost as if she didn't know what to say. When I *taxed* her with it, that is. Of course, I oughtn't to say taxed. I think *congratulate* would be right. Dear Robin will make such a *very* good husband.'

'Just how did she confess?' Although all this belonged, surely, to the larger lunacy, Carson felt that a little probing into it would he only prudent. 'What were her exact words?'

'She said, "I shall look forward to meeting your son again." Just like that.'

At this – at least metaphorically – Carson breathed more freely. Then he suddenly frowned.

'Again?' he said. 'You're sure she said *again*?'

'But of course, dear. That's the whole point, isn't it?'

'I don't see any point at all.' Carson made to pour the vodka for a second Bloody Mary, but then thought better of it. He also thought better of continuing to betray impatience. 'But, of course,' he said, 'I'm terribly interested, darling. So tell me about your whole talk with Mary Watling. Right from the start.'

'It was because she was standing in for her mother at the meeting about the bazaar. Such a *nice* girl, and so willing. We came away together, and were just passing the church when I realized the truth. Maryland, you see.'

'Maryland?'

'Robin was there for ever so long a time. Maryland, Mary Watling. You see how the truth came to me in a flash.'

Carson was silent. He didn't know that his wife had produced – and for the first time – a classical symptom of real madness. But he did realize that here, all-obscurely, was possibly a crisis on his doorstep.

'Well,' he said, 'then what? You broached the thing – is that right?'

'I said, "I'm so glad about Robin". Mary asked, "Is he coming home?" You see, I've naturally mentioned him to her before.'

'Naturally. And then?'

'I said, "Yes, of course. But what I'm really so glad about is Robin and you. Carl has always hoped that his son would marry." Mary seemed surprised. I think she was upset. She said something like, "I'm afraid I don't quite understand you."'

'Did she, indeed? Has she ever been in America?'

'Oh, yes – I knew that. She was visiting friends in Washington last year. You can ask her.'

'I don't think I'm likely to do anything of the kind.'

'Is Maryland in Washington, dear?'

'It isn't quite like that. But go on.'

'That's about all, really. Mary didn't seem anxious to announce the engagement, and I felt that perhaps I'd been tactless about it. Then she did say that about how she'd be glad to meet my son again. And then she rather hurried away.'

No doubt other people hurried away from Cynthia Carson from time to time – for example, at parties when her conversation became too perplexing to cope with. And her husband himself hurried away now. He gulped a second drink, after all, muttered something about having letters to write before dinner, slipped out of doors, and lit a cigar.

What, in heaven's name, was to be made of this development? What was the truth about it, if any truth there was, and where did Cynthia's imaginings begin? But *was* it a development? Was there any need to treat it as other than his wife's quite familiar nonsense? He saw that the answer to both these questions was, unfortunately, 'Yes'. The odd thing about the Robin business hitherto – he had to remind himself – was that Cynthia had always been so rationally persuasive about it. To what was, in fact, a tissue of untruths she customarily gave – and seemingly without effort – a convincing garment of commonplace family fact. People mightn't particularly attend to her as she chattered about her son, but neither did they ever suspect that it was a pack of lies. It was unmemorable chit-chat, but nevertheless it had built up over the years, rather in the manner of regular small payments into a deposit account, quite a substantial capital in the way of unconsidered acceptance of fantasy as fact. Carson himself – to continue the metaphor – was banking on this (or proposing so to do in just a few days' time). And now, in that luckless encounter with the Watlings' girl, Cynthia had breached this defence by extending her detectable nonsense to their nebulous son.

Or had she? It was perfectly possible to suppose that she had made up on the spur of the moment the entire conversation she had reported herself as holding with Mary Watling.

But that wasn't to be relied on. Prowling the grounds that he was so fond of recommending to the perambulations of his guests, pausing unconsciously here and there to puff cigar smoke at the greenfly on Lockett's endless rows of roses, Carson saw this clearly enough. The encounter with Miss Watling had quite probably taken place. And Cynthia, with her head already full of the imagined home-coming of her imaginary boy, had with an equal probability embarked upon it. But there was at least one plain impossibility in her account of the conversation. Mary, Cynthia asserted, had 'confessed'. But nobody can confess to being engaged to, or enamoured of, somebody who doesn't exist.

But what else was Mary asserted to have said? The answer – a vaguely reassuring one – was, 'very little'. 'I shall look forward to meeting your son again' had been the total substance of it. This needn't have been anything more than social tact. Finding herself suddenly confronted by an embarrassing delusion on the part of a woman known to be a little odd, the girl had offered this noncommittal but composing remark and then hurried away. Nothing had occurred to make her doubt the existence of Robin Carson. It was only the notion of his knowing her and being in love with her that was plainly moonshine.

So things were still not too bad. One ominous fact, nevertheless, remained. For the first time at least to his certain knowledge, Cynthia *had* talked detectable nonsense about their supposed progeny. She had only to get into the habit of doing so and Robin's entire credibility would vanish. He would become dead as a doornail in a disastrously premature fashion.

Still pacing among the roses, but now expecting at any moment to be called to dine tête-à-tête with his wife, Carson was inclined to see the woman as a viper nurtured in his bosom. This was scarcely fair. A hazard Cynthia now undeniably was. But of Robin Carson she had been, after all, the sole begetter. And without this gift to him, where would have been his marvellous plan? As a reasonable and dispassionate man, Carl Carson saw this ironic paradox clearly enough.

Lockett was working late in the garden, as he frequently did on summer evenings. He was an elderly man who had come with the house. This had been a little against Carson's inclination, since he'd have preferred a clean sweep when he bought Garford. But there had proved to be a doubt whether the man could be turned out of his cottage: it wasn't, it seemed, a 'tied' dwelling, and he might have successfully claimed the rights of a protected tenant. So it had seemed simplest to keep him in his job. Carson, who didn't know the first thing about gardening, and Cynthia, who was ignorant at least of the second, had come to rely upon him to make an adequate show. This he did admirably, and on the occasions when he worked those long hours it seemed never to occur to him to claim overtime. Oddly enough, this didn't wholly please Carson, since it had the curious effect of suggesting that much of the place was Lockett's own property. He seldom spoke of the previous owners (perhaps, Carson thought, because they had been an effete and penniless crowd) but, at the same time, it was never clear that he regarded things as looking up at Garford now that there was a Rolls in the stable. He didn't go in for the deeply spurious servility of the Punters, and although in general a somewhat crusty character he always spoke to his employer pleasantly enough. Carson, somehow, didn't greatly care for this.

Lockett was a widower, and shared his cottage with a young man called William, who was understood to be his stepson. Carson suspected William of really being a by-blow of Lockett's own. But as a broad-minded man Carson naturally took no exception to this. William was quite useful. He had employment, seemingly of an undemanding sort, in the forecourt of a service-station, and was frequently available to lend his stepfather a helping hand in a horticultural way at Garford. About the money involved here Lockett was particular, frequently naming moderate sums that the young man ought to be handed in person. On these occasions Carson would seek out William and pay up willingly enough. He sometimes wondered whether William had then to disgorge part of these gains to his stepfather towards his keep. But that was no business of his. William was lowly, and therefore – Carson supposed – not too bright. But he was a useful bundle of muscles around the place.

On his way back to the house and his dinner, Carson had a word with Lockett now. Lockett never asked gardening questions, since these were apt to leave his employer at a loss. Instead, he usually described what he was about. At the moment, he said, he was 'pegging down those Ellen Willmott verbenas'.

'Quite right, Lockett. Just the proper time for that.' Carson knew that Lockett knew that he would have said precisely this had he, Lockett, gone off his head and pursued this mysterious activity in mid-December. But conventions of this sort of knowledge on the part of a townee employer were wholly in order, and Lockett acquiesced in them. Straightening his back, he then went on to a little general conversation.

'I wouldn't care to take a liberty,' Lockett said. 'But there's been something the lad was asking me.' The 'lad' was William, and Carson had heard of William's inquiring mind before. Invoking it was, in fact, Lockett's regular technique when he had himself a problem or project to advance. 'Would you ever have thought, sir, of opening the gardens, maybe no more than a couple of times a year, in aid of the District Nursing, or such like? It was summat we did regular in the olden days.'

'Did you, indeed?' Carson prepared himself to be very short with this absurd idea.

'Miss Judith, now – that was here a few weeks back. She put me in mind of it.' Lockett had already forgotten his claim that the thought had been William's.

'And who the devil is Miss Judith?' Carson asked.

'Well, sir, it's what they've called her since almost before I knew her. Mrs Appleby. Lady Appleby, as she is today. My first employment as a garden boy was at Long Dream. The Ravens' place, sir. Lady Appleby was a Raven, as you know.'

'Ravens? I never heard of them.'

'Well, sir, that can only come of your not having been long in these parts. Quite a chat I had with Miss Judith – Lady Appleby, that is – when she and Sir John walked round the place. A noticing woman in a garden, she is – and good enough to say we ought to open the place now and then, just as we used to do at Dream.'

'I'll think about it, Lockett.' Carson had no intention of thinking about it, and judged that its having been suggested to his gardener was impertinent. But if he asserted that to Lockett, he certainly wouldn't go up in the man's estimation. Lockett was touchy, and might start, like Punter, talking about good service. He might even declare that he intended to retire, and ask his employer to take a month's notice. That would be a nuisance, particularly when Carson's mind had to be much on other things. So Carson was about to break away, when Lockett started in again. He seemed in a talkative mood.

'Very nice news, Mrs Carson has told me she's had. About her son coming on a visit. Mr Robin, isn't it – and from America? I wonder whether he has a fancy for English gardens. I've known them from those parts that have.'

'Yes, yes – but I don't know about Mr Robin, at all. We'll see, Lockett, we'll see.'

'And I suppose it will be a pleasure for you to have him, too. Rather in the same situation there – you and me, sir – in a manner of speaking.'

'Yes, we'll see.' Carson was no longer really attending to the boring Lockett – and fortunately he now heard the dinner bell. 'Good night to you, Lockett,' he said, and walked away.

But again there was that fairly rapid drop of the penny, and it almost brought Carson to a halt before he hurried on to the house. What the man had said, *exactly* what he had said, had been uncommonly odd. He had said *her son*, not *your son*. And he had declared that he and his employer were *rather in the same situation*. Carson repeated this phrase to himself, not once but several times, and saw that it was definitive; that it turned Cynthia's idle gossiping with the gardener from a mere annoyance into a definite threat.

The lad William was, or was held to be, not Lockett's son but his *stepson*, and Cynthia in talking to Lockett must have said that her son Robin was his, Carson's, *stepson* merely. There was no other way of interpreting the thing. Cynthia, after years of persuasive consistency, had started tinkering with the basic essentials of the Robin Carson myth – shoving the tedious phantom, as it were, back into a nebulous past history. Robin wasn't going to be steadily Robin *Carson* any longer. Every now and then he was to be Robin Something else.

Carson tried to tell himself that it didn't matter a damn; that his master plan wasn't affected in any way. But he knew that it was, or at least that it might be. If Robin turned *wavy* – there was no better way to express it – if he lost his simple taken-for-granted identity, his very existence, his reality-status one might say, could vanish more completely than what's-his-name's Cheshire cat. Not even a grin would be left.

Carl Carson had no doubt whatever that something disturbing had bobbed up.

7

On the following morning he rang up Pluckworthy.

'Look here,' he said, 'things are turning urgent. It's time we got down to details.'

'Details, Carl? About what?'

'About your being kidnapped, of course. And probably murdered, as well.'

'I say – hold hard!' Pluckworthy was very justifiably alarmed. 'Where are you calling from?'

'From Garford, of course. I'm in the garden.'

'The garden! How can you be telephoning from the garden? It doesn't make sense.'

'It's this cordless affair. There must be a bit of radio to it. I'm sitting in the middle of the lawn with it.'

'Christ, Carl! You ought to be sitting in the funny farm. What about that brute Punter? Are you sure he isn't lurking in the rhododendrons?'

'There aren't any. And don't waste time. I say we've got to get on with it.' As Carson said this, it did just occur to him that he had perhaps a little excessively parted with the bugging phobia. What he had now was conceivably a time phobia instead. 'I suppose,' he asked with a momentary return to common caution, 'you're alone yourself?'

'Certainly I am. Except, that is, for a spot of homework.'

'Of what? Oh, I see. Chuck her out.'

'It would be uncharitable. She's all snugged down in this very bed. Aren't you, ducks?'

'Very snug,' a female voice agreed.

'Damn your lecheries, Peter!' Carson was suddenly furious. 'Turn her out, I say, and call me back in ten minutes. And that's an order.'

'As your lordship pleases.' Pluckworthy was amused. 'And cool it, Carl, old boy. I don't mind a crazy telephone chat, if that's what you're after. It's your funeral, not mine.'

'It's certainly not yours, you young bastard.' Carson was still somewhat mindlessly incensed. 'You won't have one. If only because the body will never be found.'

'No more it will.' There was a loud crackling on the line, which was presumably the telephone's means of encoding robust laughter. 'Call you later, alligator.'

The instrument went dead, and Carson sat back in his garden chair. He cooled it. That gust of mirth, although insolent, had also been satisfactory. The more bizarre this or that aspect of the grand design, the more Pluckworthy was attracted by it. There was a trump card in that. Carson himself was inclined to be a little daunted by the very extravagance of his own conception, although he knew that it was in just that quality that its strength lay. He recalled the retired policeman – Appleford, or whatever his name had been – who had come with his stand-offish wife to Cynthia's lunch party. Could you imagine an old buffer like that having the ability to rumble so exquisite a design? The idea was ludicrous.

The telephone by Carson's side gently whistled.

'All clear,' Pluckworthy's voice said. 'So now spill the nitty-gritty.'

Carson rather disliked imported American slang. There was a decided lack of class to it. But as he was about to despatch his assistant to the United States there was no point in objecting to it now.

'You'd better be off to New York in a couple of days' time,' he said. 'No difficulty there. You won't be missed, will you?'

'Of course not. A wretch who spends half his life in bloody English trains in the interest of your rotten affairs isn't likely to be, is he?' Pluckworthy said this in quite a friendly way.

'What about that girl?'

'Girl?' Pluckworthy seemed momentarily at a loss. 'Oh, her! She has a small circle of gentlemen friends, old chap. She won't go short of conversation for a week or two.'

'It won't be a week or two – or anything like. I tell you things are urgent. The day Peter Pluckworthy flies into New York, Robin Carson flies out of it again. It's to be like that.'

'I see. Carl, you're not by any chance losing your nerve, are you?'

'Certainly not.' Carson felt a strong temptation to be furious again. 'Why the devil…'

'More haste, less speed, you know. No point in being panicked by time's winged chariot.'

'By *what*?'

'Never mind. Just my education, old boy. You're sure you've thought this thing through?'

'Of course I have.' Carson hesitated for a moment. 'Or all but. One or two dodgy points remain. Cynthia may be turning a bit awkward. There may come a point at which she needs looking after.' Carson paused again on this, but it evoked no response. He supposed that his words might have had a more sinister ring than was consciously intended, and that there were pitches on which his young assistant wouldn't play. 'Of course, no harm must come to her,' he said. 'She won't really much mind being bereft of a husband.'

'But isn't she going to be bereft of a son as well? That may upset her rather more. Robin, you know, is probably a nicer chap than Carl.'

'Damn your impudence! But, now, listen. You remember those tunnels at Heathrow?'

'In and out? Of course I do.'

'Fairly soon after you drive out, there's rather a modest roundabout. You turn off it at one point or another for the motorway to London or to the west. It's an oddly quiet little spot, and not much overlooked.'

'So that's the site of the kidnap? I see.'

'That's the site. Only, of course, it must be in the dark. If a man is to be kidnapped by nobody, it can't very well be in daylight, can it? So you must arrive at Heathrow in the small hours, hire a car…'

'Carl, I tremble for you. With the crack of the starting pistol still in our ears, you tumble straight into nonsense. Nobody arrives at Heathrow in the small hours. If you wanted darkness descending on the place with business as usual, you'd have to wait till winter comes. And by that time, of course, you'd be in the sin bin for quite a term. So think again.'

'Of course you mustn't take "small hours" too literally,' Carson said hurriedly. He saw that it was necessary to recover himself. 'Just a little dusk will do. You see…'

'Old boy, you make me tired. Take that idea of a kidnap by nobody. It's attractive – but very great nonsense, all the same. And you've thought it up merely by way of keeping your precious self out of the fracas. Well, I'm not buying it. What's the best evidence of a kidnap having taken place? The answer's simple: a short physical struggle to which there happens to be a witness or two. That's the specification we work to. Robin puts up a fight – and it's going to be with you, old chap. And there had better be some bloodshed to it.' Pluckworthy's voice had ceased to be good-humoured and whimsically tolerant. It had turned abruptly arrogant. 'I rather think,' he said, 'it will be a matter of punching you on the nose. And you can punch me back, if you like. Gore from two different blood groups will enchant the fuzz.'

'There's something in that.' Carson, although a good deal alarmed by this sudden masterful behaviour on the part of his subordinate, could not but be impressed by the bright speed of it as well. 'We must get together…'

'Tomorrow, Carl – and over lunch at that same restaurant. I'll have worked on it through the night, and got it all pat for you. I'll also have cut out breakfast, and be ready for a good feed. *Ciao*, Carl!' And Pluckworthy rang off.

Carson found himself reflecting on both these telephone conversations with a good deal of resentment. He was prepared to admit that young Pluckworthy was likely to be useful with the detail of the thing, just as he was useful in a small-scale fashion in what Carson liked to think of as his industrial empire. But the industrial empire was already virtually a thing of the past, and what was going to remain of it would be of no concern to its architect when he had disappeared into the invisibility of a harmless expatriate in Brazil or wherever. Peter Pluckworthy would be of no concern to him either; he would have served his turn, and never be privileged to come face to face with his former employer again. He would, of course, have to be left without any dangerous grievance – and that meant a substantial payment for his services. For his services – Carson reiterated to himself – in all those matters of detail.

His thought returned to the essentials: to the skeleton, the strong basic structure of the thing. Of certain aspects of this it probably wouldn't be necessary to inform Pluckworthy at all. And certainly not yet.

It could be anybody's guess that kidnappings for ransom happen, and happen successfully, more frequently than one would gather from the press. The victim's friends are always threatened with evil consequences if they contact the police; many pay up quietly; the kidnapped person is released in some unfrequented place; and that's that.

On the other hand – and this one does hear about – the criminals are caught. The police set some successful trap, baited with suitcases stuffed with bogus bank-notes or the like, and the victim is rescued more or less unharmed, although no doubt in for nightmares for a long time ahead. *But sometimes the whole thing goes wrong.* Whether under threat from the police or not, the criminals panic and throw in their hand. They vanish and are never heard of again. And occasionally their captive is never heard of again either. Perhaps he knows too much. And finally there isn't even a dead body in a ditch.

Such was to be the apparent fate of Carl Carson. Along with the ransom-money he had got together to free his son, Robin, he would have vanished for keeps. And (what was rather amusing) in a distinctly edifying way. People would say that the poor chap had met his end while behaving with the courage proper in an Englishman. And of course Robin Carson would be seen as having met a similar death at the hands of his unnerved captors. Robin's total life span would have been short – a matter, indeed, of days merely. And Peter Pluckworthy, so briefly Robin, would clearly keep his mouth shut.

That, in a nutshell, was Carson's plan. The snag, perhaps, lay in the fact that it *was* a nutshell, and that the kernel was still to find – the kernel being not only the cash that was to be raised by a distressed parent, but also the larger strategies of the several phases of the campaign. To the abduction – even the adequately sensational abduction – of young Robin Carson on his visit to England he thought he saw his way. He had to admit that it couldn't be contrived as he had originally (and elegantly) conceived it: strictly as a one-man show. With a little ingenuity, indeed, Pluckworthy *might* contrive, so to speak, to kidnap himself. But it was hard to see how such an episode could be mounted as to carry adequate conviction to sceptical minds. Without that spectacle of physical struggle which Pluckworthy had declared essential, it would be possible to believe that Robin, whether after an accident or otherwise, had simply lost his memory and was still roaming free about the land. Alternatively, it might be conjectured that he had disappeared because, for reasons unknown but probably disreputable, he had found it convenient to do so (which would be uncomfortably near the truth). Certainly people would want to pause and ask questions before organizing all that cash. And nothing could be more undesirable than that. So the charade had to be of an actual and brutal abduction carried out beneath the gaze of horrified citizens. Bloody noses would be needed, just as Pluckworthy had said. And unless accomplices were to be hazardously hired, one of the noses would indeed have to be his own.

Still, that phase of the thing could be managed. And perhaps it was the crucial phase. Violence convincingly exhibited would breed the expectation, or at least further the acceptance, of more violence in, so to speak, the same story. Mere faked evidences of a struggle *not*

61

witnessed by others might in this second instance, adequately fill the bill. A broken window, a disordered room, trampled grass, a hullabaloo in the dark contrived with deftly cut and spliced scraps of audio-tape: the possibilities of such ingenuity were virtually unlimited. And whatever was eventually fixed up, a certain amount of gore would certainly be in order.

Carson, as he told himself this, had another of his wonderful thoughts. A long time ago, he had been involved in a street accident occasioning a severe loss of blood. An emergency transfusion had been necessary, and it had almost been a disaster because his had proved to be a rare blood-group. He now saw that when it was a question of the bogus kidnapping of the non-existent Robin his own nose had better *not* be tapped. It would be too much – he felt rather confusedly – like leaving a fingerprint behind him. But of course it was different when it came to fixing up *his own* supposed abduction. When that happened, he was himself going to be prominent in the heads of those investigating the thing. So if on this occasion he arranged to leave some of his own blood on the grass, carpet, or whatever it was going to be, they'd at once ask, 'Can we tell if it may be Carson's?' At this, files would be consulted, and there would very quickly come the reply, 'Strangely enough, we can be almost certain it is.' So here actually would be a piece of refined corroborative detail!

Carson felt pleased with this train of thought, perhaps it was artlessly. He was, after all, still an amateur in crime, and he had read a good many detective stories. But the severe intellectual labour involved in fabricating such rarefied designs was fatiguing, all the same, so that at this point he broke off and took a walk into the village of Garford. It was his intention to cash a small cheque at the Post Office Stores. He had no actual need of the money, since he always kept a reasonable supply of the stuff in a drawer at home. But he was observant of the habits of others, and was aware that this was a common pottering resource of several of his propertied neighbours. The idea seemed to be that you thus suggested yourself as a modest and unassuming person, in unexpected need of a couple of pounds to pay for the milk. That Mrs Rumble, the postmistress and shopkeeper, similarly cashed cheques for the simpler classes, or would have done so had they possessed such things, Carson had never thought to discover. There were commonly two or three female villagers in the place when he went into it, but they were gossiping with Mrs Rumble and with each other rather than engaging in financial operations. On this occasion the only client or customer in the shop proved to be Colonel Watling.

The two men greeted one another with civility, although Colonel Watling's civilities were barked out in a parade ground manner. (Or so Carson felt, being unaware that colonels don't much bark out on parades.) Colonel Watling was the owner of a small estate not far from Garford House. Unlike Garford House, Upton Grange was a quite new, bogus-Cotswold-like affair, and this had made Carl Carson feel that the Carsons ought to be regarded as of greater consequence than the Watlings. But it seemed not to work out that way, perhaps because the Watlings themselves were quite old. They owned a tapestry in which an earlier Colonel Watling was being chummy with John Churchill on the field of Malplaquet, and other memorabilia of the same sort. That the Watlings were, as Carson averred, 'stuck-up' rested mainly on these evidences. Colonel Watling himself was always fairly cordial. It was said that he cherished some notion of standing for parliament in what his forbears would have called the landed interest, and he never spoke to Carson or his wife less agreeably than he did to Mrs Rumble and sundry juvenile Rumbles.

'Ha!' Watling said. 'Carson! Your son – glad to hear about it! Soon to join you – eh?'

Carson received this with mixed feelings. It was, of course, evidence of Cynthia's chattering – probably on the disturbing occasion of that encounter with Watling's daughter, Mary Watling, which Carson had already heard about. Over all such chattering there hung that air of hazard, and it made Carson wary at once. On the other hand, the spread of a persuasion that Robin was on his way was advantageous in itself. After all, Robin *was* coming home, and the more people were convinced of the fact the better. But this consideration failed quite to abate Carson's uneasiness on the present occasion. At least as Cynthia had reported it, there had been something uncommonly rum about her conversation with the Watling girl – so rum that, as we have seen, Carson had been tempted to put his faith in the supposition that Cynthia had invented the entire episode. But that seemed even more improbable now. Mary must have gone home to Upton and reported on it. Only it looked as if she had omitted the embarrassing fact that Mrs Carson imagined that she and Robin were acquainted and in love.

There was, probably, no more to it than that. Either from some well-bred reticence operative even within the family, or because it was nonsense which made Mary herself look rather ridiculous, she had curtailed Cynthia's grotesque imagining. But what if she hadn't? What if she had told the whole story, and her father was playing a deep game because unconvinced of his daughter's candour and minded to test the thing out? This was a nebulous notion – of a sort, Carson might have reflected, well calculated to illustrate the fact that it is indeed a tangled web we weave when we start in on deception.

'Yes,' he said, playing for time, 'Robin is certainly on his way back from America.' He paused to collect himself further, and then asked, 'Did your daughter, by any chance, make his acquaintance over there?'

'No! No!' The reply came from Colonel Watling as crisply as if he were rebutting an aspersion. But he immediately went on, 'Yes! Yes, I rather think she did. Girl was staying with friends in Washington, you know. Yes! Certainly!'

This was extremely upsetting – and the more so because of Watling's explosive manner. (Among his intimates, Carson had been told, he was sometimes known as the Gatling Gun.) To believing that Robin and Mary had met, whether in Washington or anywhere else, there was what must be called a totally conclusive objection, and it was tempting to regard Colonel Watling as being about as dotty as Cynthia herself. But this – Carson quickly saw – was extravagant. In Watling's inner mind all the Carsons were probably of very little account; Watling might easily get a trivial fact about one of them wrong; and it was no more than the explosive character of his speech that made this brisk contradicting of himself disconcerting. Watling had merely got things muddled. There was very little harm in that.

'Come across one day for a spot of fishing,' Watling was saying. 'Bring the lad when he turns up on you. Eh? Eh? And, of course, your wife.' This was distinctly an afterthought. 'The womenfolk always delighted to see her. Delighted!'

With this Colonel Watling gave a curt nod – conceivably a little suggestive of being directed at a subaltern – and left the post-office. For some moments Carson couldn't remember what he himself was doing in the place, and it was only after an awkward pause that he was able to ask Mrs Rumble to cash his cheque. Then he walked rather slowly back to Garford House. The Watling slant on the thing was almost certainly no more than a vexatious irrelevance. But it oughtn't to exist at all. And it worried him.

'*Petit salé aux lentilles vertes,*' Pluckworthy said easily. 'And a salad: lettuce and chicory in a walnut oil dressing, please. What about you, old boy?' Pluckworthy glanced up from the menu and took a critical look at his employer. 'Something not too fatty, I'd say. They do a very decent *Emmentaler Schafsvoressen*. And there's always their *Turospalacsinta*, although it's sometimes served not quite hot enough.'

'I'll have turkey,' Carson said rather shortly. 'And I don't see…'

'*Filetti di tacchino alla nerone* for the gentleman,' Pluckworthy said. 'The wine list, please.'

As Carson would once more be footing the bill – to say nothing of subsequently feeing his fellow-conspirator – he justly resented thus being taken charge of in the restaurant. If he didn't have a care, he told himself, the young man would soon be running the show. So when the wine had been chosen he spoke out.

'We'll have nothing written down about this,' he said. 'Not so much as a scribble in a notebook or diary. That's my first instruction to you. Just remember it. Everything's to be under your hat.'

'But I haven't got a hat.' Pluckworthy was amused. 'And I doubt whether Robin has one either. Not that your point isn't sound enough in its elementary way. And to show that I'm quite clear-headed, we'll begin with a recap.'

'We'll begin just as I…'

'Listen, for a start, to the heads of the thing. I fly to New York. I change into Robin Carson, and fly back here. You don false whiskers, or whatever, and kidnap me in some noticeable way. Still being, in fact, a free agent, I withdraw into a loo or similar place of seclusion, turn into myself again, and walk out with a certain sum in used banknotes in my pocket. And *right* out. I have nothing further to do with the thing.'

'I haven't decided about that.' Carson failed to say this very robustly. He could see – although, oddly enough, it was a fresh perception – that Pluckworthy need not, it was true, bear any further functional part in the conspiracy. Unfortunately he was coming to rely on the young man, so that the thought of being on his own so early in the affair was disagreeable to him. He also had an obscure notion that it would be prudent to involve Pluckworthy in rather more than the mere peccadillo of having agreed to cross the Atlantic under an assumed name. He ought to be provided with a more substantial reason for keeping his mouth shut.

'I haven't decided,' he amplified, 'about the point at which you'll have earned your keep. I may have some further use for you. And, in any case, you'd better be clear about the rest of the plan.'

'I am – and it can be put in a few sentences. You raise money to ransom your supposed son. The supposed kidnappers supposedly panic or perhaps double-cross you.' Pluckworthy paused for a moment on this. 'They supposedly double-cross you first, and nobble both you and your cash. *Then* they supposedly panic, and in some never-to-be-disclosed hole there are supposedly two Carson corpses. It's a shade, macabre, is it not? But so is the sequel: Carl Carson living out a furtive and purposeless life somewhere amid a crowd of dagoes. Any comment?'

'Two comments, Peter.' Carson pulled himself together, and endeavoured to maintain a firm line. 'The first being simply that I don't like your tone.'

'As not being what ought to obtain between gentlemen? You make me laugh. And the second?'

'The second is that I value your advice, my dear Peter.' Carson contrived to suggest a positive warmth of regard as he made this capitulation. 'Over every stage of the thing. Just continue to give your mind to it, and I'll make the cash half as much again.'

'Double.'

'Double.'

'The fact is, Carl, that you don't really *see* it. The large and nebulous conception, yes. The concrete action, or series of actions, no.'

'You mean the details. I'll admit there's some truth in what you say.'

'Good. I said I'd work it all out. And I have.' Pluckworthy paused again, this time to apply himself to a dish the honest name for which was pickled pork. 'I can go through it in ten minutes. Just listen.'

And Carl Carson listened.

PART TWO

JOHN APPLEBY

8

'Those people at Garford,' John Appleby said. 'I suppose we ought to be asking them to lunch or dinner.'

'I've had it in mind,' Judith Appleby said.

'A bit out of turn, their inviting us first. But still.'

'As you say, but still.' Lady Appleby was always amused by her husband's sense of the social punctilios. 'One must be civil to one's neighbours.'

'Do you know, Judith, that I don't think I'd call the Carsons neighbours – simply because I can't see their chimneys from the top of the house? What constitutes one's neighbourhood is an expansible and contractible concept.'

'What a very philosophical idea! As a matter of fact, I encountered Mrs Carson yesterday. It was in Busby's shop in Linger. She was trying to buy linen sheets, and rather creating because they hadn't any.'

'Quite right. Surely a linen-draper ought to have no end of linen sheets in his shop.'

'Busby's shop – *linen*?'

'Well, yes. We sleep between linen sheets, don't we?'

'Certainly we do. But they're as old as the hills. I cherish them as I cherish the Sèvres. Incidentally, I had the feeling I mentioned to you after the Carsons' party. That the woman is a bit off her head. She had quite a lot to say to me, as well as to Mr Busby, about needing new sheets for her blue room. She kept on about her blue room, and eventually she explained that she was getting it ready for her son.'

'Robin Carson. I remember about him. They go over and visit him at sweet little Key Biscayne.'

'That's right – but now Robin has arrived in England. Mum had a telephone call from him at Heathrow a few evenings previously, to say he was hiring a car and would be on his way to Garford. But he didn't turn up, and hadn't turned up yesterday. I suppose his courage had failed him before the prospect of the family hearth. The poor lady was relieved in a way – about the delay, I mean. It gave her an opportunity to go after sheets and things. But she was beginning to be anxious as well. And she said her husband had gone quite tense and jumpy.'

'Then perhaps we'd better hold our hand about inviting them until the dilatory Robin has been restored to their bosom. Of course we'll have to ask him as well.' Appleby paused on this. 'I remember her as being quite sensible about their son. But definitely a bit dotty in some other regions of discourse.'

'You sometimes sound a bit dotty yourself, John. Regions of discourse, indeed! The Carsons struck me as not having a single general idea between them. It would have been a frightfully boring occasion if Humphry and that nice wife of his hadn't been there.'

'The Lelys undoubtedly saved us. Which reminds me that I saw Humphry the other day, and he said he'd been painting Carson's portrait. What about your getting a commission to do Mrs C in bronze?'

'It's a thought.' Judith Appleby, who was a sculptor (or sculptress) seemed unenthusiastic before this idea. 'Have you discovered anything much about Carson himself?'

'No – and I can't say I've tried. Arthur Watling – who's Carson's neighbour in my modest sense of the term – has mentioned him to me once or twice. Arthur called him a clever little city chap. For Arthur "clever" is quite as dismissive a word as "little", don't you think? It's my impression that Carson is pretty prosperous in what's possibly a ramshackle way. Share-pushing type. Promotes things.'

'He belongs, in fact, to the great entrepreneurial class. I wonder whether Robin follows in his footsteps.'

'You can ask the young man himself, when he finally turns up and is introduced to us.'

'I suppose he *will* turn up?'

Lady Appleby had produced this question abruptly and as if it rather surprised her. Sir John Appleby, who was about to enter upon his daily half-hour with *The Times,* put the paper down again on the breakfast-table.

'Ah!' he said.

'The woman was surely quite right to be worried about the non-appearance of her son. He telephones that he has arrived, and then no more is heard of him. One can think of various explanations, some of them merely undutiful. For instance, he may have suddenly gone off after a promising girl. But if I were the Carsons, I'd be ringing round the hospitals.'

'Carson may well have done that, without alarming his wife by telling her. She may be a little mad, but he's quite sane and competent. And if he did so and drew a blank, an accident or sudden illness isn't the explanation, since it's almost impossible to imagine anything of the kind that could bring in a casualty there was no means of identifying.'

'Robin might have been robbed, and stripped of anything carrying his name, and be in a coma.'

'Good heavens, Judith, what a macabre imagination you have! A hospital with that on its hands – and there's probably not a single such case in all England at this moment – doesn't let any inquirer get away without a come-look-see. It's long odds against the missing Robin being anywhere of the sort.'

'Then where is he?'

'It's a good question.' Appleby didn't say this with much enthusiasm. 'Do you know my bet? He took one look at England in this present year of Grace, and bolted back to the USA.'

'I don't see that as in the least plausible, John. If Robin Carson is a hypersensitive type, he might certainly back hastily out of England. But it wouldn't be from a deplorable frying-pan into an equally deplorable fire.'

'Out of the frying-pan of Paynim rites into the fire of Mahometry.' Appleby in retirement passed the time with much miscellaneous reading. 'He'd probably try Kamchatka or the South Pole.'

But later that morning Appleby found himself again thinking about the missing Robin Carson. Just why he did so, he didn't clearly know. Many years before, and when cutting that unusual path for himself through the CID to the surprising elevation of Commissioner of Metropolitan Police, he had been a good deal concerned from time to time with missing persons. Perhaps that was it. But just lately Garford House and its inhabitants had interested him too. Judith had been interested in the gardener, who had worked at Long Dream as a boy. He himself had taken notice of the butler, in whom he recognized a criminal type, hopefully reformed. But the employers of these people had attracted a larger speculation. Carl Carson was somehow rather more than just a scantily educated tycoon. Much in him had been commonplace – as when he had been quick to reveal, or pretend, that he was familiarly acquainted with the Lord Mayor of London, or had – to Judith's quite improper amusement – described as his 'grounds' certain large stretches of lawn interspersed with rectangular beds overfilled with uninteresting modern roses. But, if elusively, there was a strong dash of enterprise in Carson. Commercial enterprise, no doubt. But also, in sudden far-away looks, a hint of something potentially more freakish in that area. He was the sort of man – Appleby told himself – who might one day notice, say, a fire-balloon drifting overhead, and within a fortnight achieve a corner in the manufacture of the things. Fellows with that sort of facility were likely to amass quite a packet in the bank. They were also liable to come a cropper. To come a cropper and bob up again. Carson wasn't a nice man. Probably he wasn't at all a nice man. But there was a good deal there, all the same.

As for Mrs Carson – so ineptly christened Cynthia – her silliness was of an almost endearing kind. 'A little mad' was no doubt a fair description of her now, although a mad doctor might describe her as no more than neurotic. It was probable that she would eventually go downhill, so that if she had the misfortune to reach her eighties it would be in a state of senile dementia. Appleby felt he had met such Cynthias in old age before – and commonly amid the sort of family misfortunes that lie on the fringes of crime. The Carsons' son, although for some reason long resident in the USA, could be felt as her mainstay in point of an undistorted sense of reality. So if Robin was currently engaged in more or less ditching his parents – whether in favour of metal more attractive or for any other reason – he was a thoroughly unfilial and blameworthy young man.

Thus did Sir John Appleby, a senior citizen tolerably well-seen in human nature, meditate dispassionately on the Carsons of Garford House. He was, as it happened, still doing so when a Rolls-Royce appeared unexpectedly on the drive. When it drew up before the front door it was Carl Carson who stepped out of it. For some seconds Appleby was far from pleased. He supposed that the awkward chap was paying what he'd dimly think of as a courtesy call. But this, he at once decided, was a false scent. Carson's son had disappeared, and Carson, aware of the eminence from which Appleby had retired, had come to seek his advice. That must be it. It wasn't a development Appleby exactly relished. But he reflected that the man might well be in considerable distress, and he hurried out to be properly welcoming.

'I thought I'd just drop in on you,' Carson said.

'Very nice of you, my dear Carson. Do sit down. Judith will be delighted.'

This last was an unnecessary, and even slightly excessive assurance. When a man turns up on one, there is no call hastily to declare the enchantment of one's wife. But Carson seemed pleased.

'Cynthia,' he said with a certain solemnity, 'had the pleasure of running into Lady Appleby yesterday.'

'Ah, yes – so Judith has told me. Mrs Carson spoke of your son, and of your expecting a visit from him.'

'Just so. And we're a little surprised, as a matter of fact, that Robin hasn't yet turned up on us. But there's nothing out of the way about it; nothing out of the way, at all.' Carson offered this information not so much easily as airily. 'Boys will be boys, wouldn't you say?'

Literally received, this appeared to be a glimpse of the obvious, and its application in a larger sense to Robin Carson's non-appearance at Garford was, at least as yet, not for Appleby to comment upon. So he remained silent.

'Only, you see, my wife is a little nervous about Robin,' Carson pursued. 'I don't know whether you noticed the fact, but she's decidedly of a nervous type. Highly strung, as they say. A splendid creature, Appleby, but undeniably highly strung.'

This again was a shade difficult to respond to. It did seem fairly clear to Appleby that about Carson himself there hung a distinctly nervous air. And about this there was something indefinably complex. Was the man in a state of anxiety which for some reason – perhaps a notion of proper manly behaviour – he felt obliged to dissimulate? And was he conceivably off-loading this anxiety on his wife? There was a small puzzle here – but Appleby told himself it was a puzzle he felt no particular impulse to resolve.

'It's no doubt natural,' he said, 'that Mrs Carson should be a little worried if your son has failed to turn up on an expected date.'

'Exactly that. And, of course, it's all nonsense. Young people are so thoroughly independent nowadays, wouldn't you say? Robin will judge a few days to be neither here nor there. He probably has a fish or two of his own to fry in London before coming down to dull old Garford.'

'It's fortunate that you feel no unreasonable anxiety in the matter yourself, Carson. You must be the better able to reassure your wife.' But as Appleby said this he continued to be aware that Carson's nonchalance was assumed. The man's wife had told Judith that he was tense and jumpy, and so he really was. Yet that didn't quite adequately describe the thing. It was almost as if, despite everything he said, Carson was designing to be detected as beset by apprehensions. And why, if he was really not worried about his son, had he turned up at Long Dream now? It could scarcely be, as Appleby had at first imagined, to seek more or less professional advice on how to track down a missing person. But now Carson himself offered an explanation of this.

'I've been rather afraid,' he said, 'that when Cynthia met Lady Appleby yesterday she may have given the impression that there is really some cause for alarm about Robin. But, as I've said, it just isn't so. And I wouldn't like Lady Appleby to feel worried about it. Which is why I've called, you see, to say a reassuring word.'

Appleby was again silent for a moment. It wasn't easy to see how to cope civilly with this absurdity. For an absurdity it was. Judith would have to be a person of quite morbid sensibility were she to be thrown into a state of distress by the non-arrival at his parents' dwelling of a totally strange young man. Carl Carson was no doubt a somewhat egocentric chap, inclined to believe that his affairs made more impact on others than in fact they did. But the notion he had just advanced was rather dotty, all the same. Perhaps he had picked up a streak at least of eccentricity from his wife.

'I think Judith must be out around the place,' Appleby said. 'But, of course, I'll tell her what you say. I'm sure she'll be relieved.' Appleby paused on this untruth, and then added another. 'It has been extremely kind of you to call.'

'I'm only sorry I must hurry away.' Carson got to his feet as he made this handsome response. 'As it happens, I have a good deal on hand at the moment. Really a great deal on hand.' This time, the man was openly agitated. 'It happens in business every now and then, you know. Quite suddenly, there's such pressure on one from this and that that one hardly knows how to find the time for it all.'

'Then it's the kinder of you to have run over to Dream,' Appleby said with dishonest heartiness. At least the man did seem to be going away.

'And it's easy to get flurried on such occasions – and find that the more haste the less speed. The feeling that time is running out before things are properly fixed up. But perhaps, Appleby, it hasn't been within your experience – anything, I mean, of that sort. Anyway, I'm off to town. Driving up. Can't spare the time for that damned train.'

This sudden obsession with the *tempus fugit* aspect of things lasted until Carson was actually at the wheel of his car. 'And I'm driving myself,' he then went on. 'Punter's a damn sight too slow. My regards to your good lady, Appleby.' And with this no doubt proper expression Carl Carson might be said to have shot suddenly out of sight. Only a slight cloud of dust on the drive of Dream Manor remained as a token of his visit.

Appleby turned to go back into the house, and found Judith at his shoulder.

'Was that the man Carson?' she asked.

'Yes, it was.'

'Asking for your help?'

'Well, no. Or not exactly. I thought it was going to be that – because of his son's failure to turn up, and the fuss his wife is in as a result. But it didn't seem to be quite that. The fellow had a cock-and-bull story about wanting to relieve your mind of any worry his Cynthia may have caused you by her talk in Busby's shop. Sheer moonshine. And he wasn't, as I say, asking for help. Rather he came to tell me something – or perhaps just to hint at something or set something stirring in my head. The lord knows why, and I almost feel the man's up to no good. Incidentally, I said you'd be delighted to see him.'

'Did you, indeed!'

'And he sent you his compliments as he drove off. I said you were probably messing around, and unaware that he was here.'

'I was on the telephone, as a matter of fact. Answering a call. It was from his wife.'

'The thing's a persecution! Just what did she want?'

'She *did* want help. She asked to speak to the Commissionaire, and I said he was engaged – which was true enough.' For many years it had been one of Judith Appleby's tasks to head off importunate demands for her husband's attention.

'Did she know her husband was over here?'

'I don't think she did. It was her line that he was worried off his head by Robin's vanishing, but I feel that she herself is really the one most disturbed about it. She said something about Robin's romance making it so certain he'd want to come home. The young man is more or less engaged, she seemed to imply, to the Watlings' girl, Mary.'

'The people at the Grange? I don't see how this Robin…'

'He and Mary met in America, it seems. It was all a little obscure and scatty. You remember the poor woman is like that. But she was sure you could help in some way.'

'I see.' Appleby, although indisposed to view the Carsons in a particularly sympathetic light, received this soberly. 'So what can be done? Probably nothing much at the moment, except trying to get these people clear in one's head. They themselves seem to be in a bit of a muddle, and it's possible there isn't a normal husband-and-wife relationship of confidence between them.'

'You'd say that's the normal thing?'

'I've always assumed so, although perhaps on rather a narrow basis of experience. But stick to the point. The woman's the easier of the two to size up – although one has to allow for the fact that she's a bit mad and may be prone to imagine things. She's in a tizzy because this Robin has gone astray; she sees, or believes, that her husband is in a tizzy too; and she remembers that she has lately made the acquaintance of a kind of great detective or top policeman. She tries to enlist this chap's help. All that's simple enough.'

'So it is. Particularly the great-detective part.'

'The man's more difficult. He presents himself here in a most unnecessary way to assure us there's nothing to worry about, and that he himself is quite easy in his mind about the tardiness of friend Robin. But, quite patently, he's in a tizzy as well – just as his wife says he is. In an obscure way, he almost obtrudes the fact. And time is in some equally obscure way an enemy. He's having to rush around, apparently on business occasions having presumably nothing to do with the Robin crisis. That's about it.'

'I suppose so.' Judith took a moment to weigh this summary. 'Carson drove over here to create an impression.'

'Yes.'

'Why on us? We scarcely know the people. It's the great detective factor again.'

'Allowing, Judith, for the satirical slant of your mind, that must be about the truth. It's not just that he wants to create an impression. He wants to start a train of thought along what one may call professional lines. It's really uncommonly odd, and I can't say I make much of it.' Appleby said this with a touch of genuine impatience, and Judith could see that he believed himself far from anxious to get absorbed in anything that could be called the Carson mystery.

'What about the lady's plea for help?' she asked.

'Well, yes – one oughtn't to ignore such things. But a missing person is very much a matter for the police. They have the machinery – and it's probably not very like the machinery in my time. The problem is a sizeable one, you know. The number of persons who can be described as missing in this country at any one time has to be reckoned by the thousand. It requires evidence of there being crime in the picture to set the machine at all effectively in motion.'

'And there's nothing of the sort in Robin Carson's picture.'

'So far as we know, nothing at all. It's my bet that the young man will simply turn up – perhaps leaving something rather discreditable behind him.'

'So that's that.' Judith Appleby knew that when her husband came out with a rather heavy remark of this sort he was intending to dismiss a topic from his mind. She rather suspected, nevertheless, that he would in fact continue to do some thinking about the tiresome Carsons and their elusive son.

9

For some days, however, nothing of the sort happened. Somewhat sporadically at this time, Appleby was writing a book. It wasn't autobiographical, and such sensational crimes as it touched on had occurred for the most part in the fourteenth and fifteenth centuries. Appleby had taken to that investigating and recording of local history which has become prominent as an unassuming pursuit among the elderly and literate classes. When questioned about it, he would say that it served as well as the bees. This was understood to be an allusion to the final phase in the career of Sherlock Holmes.

It was an activity having the advantage of requiring very little equipment. A typewriter, a filing cabinet, a magnifying glass (Sherlockian in suggestion) and plenty of hot water filled the bill: this last because of the decidedly dusty condition of such minor archives as commonly came his way. He might, indeed, have added to the need for plenty of hot water (together with soap and towels) the need for plenty of petrol as well. Appleby drove around the countryside a good deal. He was doing so on the day we resume our acquaintance with him. Having lunched agreeably on bread and cheese with an aged clergyman at Boxer's Bottom, and been by him alerted to the possibility of interesting discovery in the parish registers at Sleep's Hill, he was making his way to the latter rural centre over rather unfrequented roads when he became aware of something amiss with the ancient Appleby Rover. He drew to a halt, and found he had a puncture.

Appleby was displeased. Casual observation had convinced him that punctures, like some of the less important diseases, simply didn't happen to people nowadays. And if the car was old, its tyres were reasonably new.

It was a vexatious situation, but had to be dealt with. Appleby took his jacket off and yanked the tool kit out of the boot. But then, glancing along the deserted road ahead, he became aware of some sort of garage or service station a couple of hundred yards away. What a mechanic could achieve in minutes, he saw no occasion himself to labour at. Standing on his years, he'd hand the job over to a professional. It wasn't exactly an athletic decision, but this didn't perturb him.

Then for a moment it looked as if he were going to draw a blank. In the garage there didn't seem to be much going on, and ominously erected beside it was a large notice saying 'For Sale'. But the situation turned out to be not so bad as it seemed. Nothing, indeed, that could be called an activity was visible. But a young man in blue dungarees sat perched on an oil-barrel under another notice which read 'No Smoking'. Perhaps by way of declaring his independence of the moribund establishment employing him, he was puffing at a cigarette. He was presumably willing to sell petrol. He could probably be persuaded to change a wheel.

This proved to be so. The young man clearly expected no more business for his firm that day, and it was presumably as a citizen rather than an employee that he would eventually name a fee for his services to Appleby. He provided himself with the superior sort of jack that trundles along on wheels, and set off for the Rover. He was an alert-seeming young man with an observant eye, but at present so obviously sunk in gloom that Appleby expected no conversation from him.

'Appleby, isn't it?' the young man asked.

'Yes, my name's Appleby.' Appleby was unoffended by the egalitarian cast of this question. 'What's yours?'

'William.'

'There doesn't seem to be much doing here, William. You must find it a bit dull.'

'Dump is closing down at the end of the week. Ever since I've been here, I've felt the undertakers and gravediggers to be raring to get busy on it. And the job's been no more than part-time, anyway. Now I'm out on my bloody ear.'

'I'm sorry to hear that. By the way, how do you come to know my name's Appleby?'

'My dad – a step-dad, he is really – worked at Long Dream, come he was a lad. Name of Jim Lockett. I call myself William Lockett, it being easier that way. Dad has pointed you out to me. Your missis, too, who was born in the place, he says.'

'So she was. Does your dad work somewhere else now?'

'Gardener at Garford he's been, these thirty years or more. For the old lot there, and now for the new – name of Carson, never known in these parts before. I help out at times around the place. Ruddy moonlighting, really. But I can quite take gardening. Learnt a packet about it, too, from dad. I'd sooner cart muck all day than go messing around with this grease and stinking petrol... Your car looks like it might have come out of Noah's Ark.'

'Twenty years ago, William, they knew how to make cars to last.' Appleby produced this senior citizen's platitude with confidence. 'What about Mr Carson at Garford taking you on full-time to help your dad? Wealthy, isn't he? And he could do with an under-gardener, what with all those roses.'

'You make me laugh.' William Lockett scowled as he said this, and applied himself viciously to the nuts on the peccant wheel. 'What about Long Dream?' he asked suddenly. 'You wouldn't have a job going there? I'm not all that bloody useless.'

Appleby, who had just decided that – so strange were the times – a couple of pound coins would be the decent thing to slip to the lad for his fifteen minute's work, realized that this small occasion had taken on a new dimension. A young man with the dole queue dead ahead of him had shown the kind of enterprise of which one ought to approve. It had to be treated with respect and responded to with care.

'I'm afraid not,' Appleby said at once. 'You see, we have Mr Hoobin – your father may remember him – and also a lad called Solo. Of course Mr Hoobin is elderly, and Solo is about as useful as a garden gnome. But there they are. I could possibly do you a day a week, and see how you all got on. But you'd want something more than that.'

'It wouldn't be exactly a living – would it?' With a deft tug, William pulled the wheel from its hub. 'But thanks for the idea.'

'Mightn't it start you on something, William? There must be an increasing number of people in these parts with fair-sized gardens, who can't run to help in them for more than a day in the week or the fortnight…'

'Distressed gentry, like.' The spare wheel was now in place. 'A quid an hour, and a cup of tea.'

'You'd have to get together your own tools – including one or two power-tools. Power-tools always impress distressed gentry. Not too difficult, that. And then there's only one further step, and it's no doubt the tricky one. Organize your transport.'

'A pram, maybe. Sometimes you see a tramp going along with one of them.' William was now being his own power tool as he twisted the nuts tight with the simple implement known as a spider.

'But you won't be a tramp. You'll be a garden contractor.'

'Jack down the crate, and another turn on the nuts. If the pressure's right in your spare, you're on the road… I'll say you talk more sense than some.' For the first time, William hesitated a little. 'You'll be over this way again?'

'Probably not for quite some time. If you're interested, come to Dream one morning, and we'll have another word about it. But no commitments.'

'I'll think.' William uttered this as one who makes a handsome concession. He had disengaged the jack, and given a ritual kick at the spare tyre. 'That's a quid,' he said.

Appleby handed over the quid. To add a second would, he decided, be an act of possibly offensive benevolence. He then realized that his zeal in thinking up a career for William Lockett had caused him to pass over a point of some interest in their discussion.

'By the way,' he said, 'why should my suggesting that Mr Carson might take you on full-time strike you as funny? It seems a perfectly reasonable idea to me – particularly as you and your father are used to working together.'

'What do you know? The man's clean busted – just as much as this bloody service station.'

'Busted? Who are you talking about?'

'Carson, of course. That bastard of a butler told my dad there's not a doubt about it. All sudden-like. The Rolls went yesterday. And the day before, Punter says, it was some of the pictures. Carson told him they were going to be cleaned. I ask you! Who ever heard of cleaning pictures – like they might be your best pants? Bankrupt, that's your Carson. Full time, indeed! Like enough, it's what he himself will be doing in clink.'

Appleby considered this surprising communication on its merits. They scarcely seemed substantial merits. Pictures do get cleaned. If of sufficient importance, they are sometimes lent to galleries and exhibitions. Even Rolls-Royces have to be serviced. Or one may be taken away in order that, a few days later, an even grander one may take its place. Carson was probably not very popular with his retainers. Marked prosperity emanating from a mysterious region of intricate financial operations was liable to be suspect alike to sophisticated and unsophisticated intelligences. And so on. William might very well be talking nonsense. But Appleby found himself not very confident about this. And if Carson's peace of mind was simultaneously under threat from two quarters – this of looming business disaster on top of the disappearance of his son – his very evident unease would be amply accounted for.

'Dad will be all right,' William was saying as he wiped his hands on a cotton rag. 'If he's as careful as hell, that is. His pension's coming along, and he has a bit put by. But it won't exactly be two at the pub.'

'All the more reason for thinking about what I've said.' Appleby spoke briskly as he got into his car. 'And thank you very much for your help.'

Driving on, Appleby found himself rather puzzled by his own behaviour. William Lockett was probably a decent enough lad, deserving of the chance of continued employment. But Appleby was not by temperament any sort of travelling philanthropist, so how was his interest in the young man to be explained? The answer proved not hard to find. What was operative in him wasn't an interest in William at all. It was an interest in the Carsons of Garford House, and anything he could hear about them. Almost without being conscious of the fact, he had developed a considerable curiosity in that direction. But there was something more positive to it than that. Obscurely, but insistently, he had a sense of having failed to put two and two together. And that was something that a detective – even in retirement and much taken up with the complexities of local history – ought not to do.

On the remainder of the drive to Dream Appleby pursued these unsatisfactory thoughts. During that final phase of his career in which he had administered the Metropolitan Police his wife had sometimes made fun of what she called his retentive nose for a mystery. It had been fair enough, since he had undeniably devoted a good deal of diplomatic skill to masking a continuing and unseemly interest in mere murder and mayhem. And the impulse was with him still. In the rural seclusion in which he now lived sensational crime was undeniably in short supply. But what might be called puzzles did turn up. Carl Carson was lodging himself in Appleby's head as a puzzle of sorts – and as a result Appleby had taken on at least a small domestic problem. The notion of recruiting William Lockett to back up the horticultural efforts of the aged Hoobin and his nephew Solo was perfectly rational in itself – yet he had to acknowledge that it simply wouldn't have occurred to him if William Lockett hadn't happened to live with his stepfather at Garford. The gardens at Dream weren't what they had been once upon a time; the topiary, for example, had gone; the tennis-court, now seldom in use, had turned bumpy. But quite a lot was in reasonable order, and considerable labour was required to keep it so. He supplied a good deal himself, but nevertheless Hoobin was perhaps entitled to be helped out a little more than he was. Hoobin, however, was himself the small domestic problem. He might take a dark view of young Lockett. Appleby was reflecting on this as he turned the Rover into his drive. Fifty yards on, he had to pull up sharply.

This was because of Solo. Solo was standing in the middle of the drive, his body canted forward in the effort to edge a Dutch hoe through a clump of dandelions. Or that was how it looked. But Solo, of course, was asleep. Falling asleep in unlikely postures and amid abrupted activities was Solo's forte. Hoobin, although expending much energy on loudly dratting the boy when he was awake, stoutly maintained that his nephew's precarious health necessitated the utmost caution on his employers' part when they judged it essential to rouse the youth from his slumbers. Appleby, whose instincts were always humane, at times indulged this view of the matter. So he climbed out of the Rover now, advanced upon the virtually Ephesian sleeper, and laid a cautious hand upon his shoulder.

'Solo,' he said gently, 'wake up.'

Rather surprisingly, Solo woke up at once. For some seconds he glanced at Appleby vacantly and without expression. Then – faintly but unmistakably – his features took on a look of malicious glee. (This – Appleby was accustomed to remark – constituted the only reliable evidence that Solo and Hoobin were indeed in some blood-relationship.)

'Cump'ny', Solo said with relish.

'What's that?'

'Cump'ny – up at house.'

'Oh, I see.' In relation to Long Dream Manor and all its policies both Hoobin and Solo indulged extreme territorial feelings. All visitors were intruders and a disaster – and this view they never doubted was that of their employers too. So Solo now regarded himself as enjoying the satisfaction of conveying ill tidings.

'Do you know who they are?' Appleby asked. Solo shook his head, and then his eyes appeared about to close again. Appleby gently possessed himself of the hoe, dealt with the dandelions, and carefully restored Solo to an approximately perpendicular posture. 'Carry on,' he said encouragingly. And he got back into the Rover.

He put the car away in its garage and walked towards the house – wondering, although without the gloom taken for granted by Solo, who had called. Hoobin, as usual, was sitting by the door of his potting shed. The hour having drawn on towards teatime, Hoobin (always, as he liked to describe himself, a perusing man) had advanced far into his diurnal task of consuming the *Daily Mirror*. Politics, pugilism, the varying fortunes of race horses – all of them topics upon which he was completely ignorant – he had fingered his way through with equal care. So he could afford the diversion of articulate speech.

'Cump'ny', Hoobin said.

'So Solo has told me. Do you know who they are?'

'Furriners.'

For a moment Appleby had the agreeable thought that he was perhaps being visited by *confrères* retired from the *Sûreté nationale*. Then he recalled that, just as Judith regarded as neighbours any persons of substance within half a day's journey of Long Dream Manor, so did Hoobin regard as foreigners the entire human race not actually resident in the tiny hamlet of Long Dream itself. Appleby had never, indeed, heard Hoobin speak, like rustics in Thomas Hardy, of the distant kingdom of Bath. But had he mentioned that he had that day visited both Boxer's Bottom and Sleep's Hill (to say nothing of having passed through Snarl, Sneak, and Little London) Hoobin would indubitably regard it as an expedition as recklessly far-flung as that announced in the opening lines of the *Odyssey*.

'Do you know any of them?' Appleby asked – perhaps wondering whether the company was one into which he must hasten.

'Parson.'

'But you wouldn't call Dr Folliott a foreigner, Hoobin?'

'All parsons be a bit aside from folk. And there's one o' they from Upton. T'wench, it be. And the artist-creature and his wife that visit times enough.'

'Mr and Mrs Lely, you mean?' Appleby wondered whether Hoobin ought to be reproved for calling Humphry Lely an artist-creature, but decided that nothing markedly derogatory had been intended.

'Them it be. And all sitting under the cedar on lawn. A dangerous tree, that cedar's coming to be.' Hoobin offered this information with gloomy satisfaction. 'Biding their tea, all of them. And parson maybe thinking to wait on for something else.'

'Well, I must go and join them.' Appleby had again considered the propriety of rebuking Hoobin for this last aspersion, and had concluded that it would be injudicious to do so. Moreover, there was a bull to take by the horns. 'Hoobin,' he asked, 'do you know a young man called William Lockett?'

'Old Lockett be beknown to me – we being colleagues here afore your time, Sir John.' Stray words culled from his perusals occasionally filtered into Hoobin's vocabulary. 'Along o' Heyhoe.'

'I knew Heyhoe, Hoobin. Although not for long. And Spot.'

'Spot? The dratted creature that was for ever casting a shoe.'

'So he was, Hoobin. Old times, those.' Appleby felt that he had now successfully chatted up his aged gardener, and might proceed to the nub of the matter. 'William Lockett is old Mr Lockett's stepson.'

'So he be. But I take no account o' stepsons. Queer cattle, times enough, Sir John. Unholy incest be at the back o' them, often as not.'

'This young William Lockett has picked up a little gardening at Garford.' Appleby chose to ignore the serious moral issue upon which Hoobin was plainly minded to advance. 'And now he may be looking for occasional work that way elsewhere. He's probably coming over to talk to me about it.' Appleby paused on this, but the information was received in ominous silence. 'He might make it easier for Solo.'

'What that Solo needs is the taking of a switch to him. Not that I han't leathered his arse often enough.' Hoobin produced this perhaps mildly exaggerated statement of his domestic sanctions and sanctities with complete confidence. 'But the poor weevil creature will keep falling asleep. And then it's dangerous.'

The Applebys having obtained medical opinion discounting this apprehension, Appleby thought it unnecessary to enter upon it now.

'You can have a word with this William yourself, Hoobin,' he said, 'and judge whether he seems sober and reliable. You're a man who notices such things.'

'That I be.' Hoobin was plainly mollified. But then he rallied. 'Happen he can scythe?' he asked.

'I didn't ask him. But I'd suppose not. There are few left that have your skill with a scythe, Hoobin. Solo can't scythe.'

'Give Solo a scythe!' Hoobin was horrified. 'Afore you looked, he'd have the legs off a centipede – and his own as well. Carting muck in a barrow: that's what I'll set your young Lockett to.'

'It's something he particularly likes. The stink of the stuff, he says, isn't as bad as the stink of petrol. A part-time job in a garage has packed up on him.'

'I'll try him, Sir John.' Hoobin was suddenly magnanimous. 'Things being that bad there at Garford with them unholy Carsons.'

'Things bad at Garford, Hoobin?' Appleby asked this sharply. 'Just what do you mean by that?'

'Every penny gone, they say, and the bailiffs like to move in at any time. It's right enough this lad should be looking to himself.'

'Have you any evidence for that?' It seemed remarkable to Appleby that here should be the same presage of improbably drastic doom at Garford House as he had received little more than an hour ago from William Lockett himself. But he knew that Hoobin did of an evening frequent the Raven Arms in the village. The gossip of the folk would become quickly known to him.

'And fair's fair,' Hoobin went on, unheeding. 'It mayn't be the Carson-body's fault, for all I know. Not with all them crooks and cheats in stock exchanges and such like places. What with it coming all that bad, the lad William deserves his chance. I'll try him, that I will. For I'm an open-minded man, I am. And it's the perusing does it, Sir John.' Upon this elevating thought, Hoobin picked up his *Daily*

Mirror again. 'There do seem to have been a terrible great child-murder in Houndsditch,' he said. 'There be a whole column on it. I've been reading about it, I have, this half hour and more.'

'Then I mustn't hold you up,' Appleby said. And he went to join his guests beneath the perilous cedar of Lebanon.

10

The first person Appleby noticed on the lawn was Mary Watling. He didn't know her – or, indeed, any of the family at Upton Grange – very well. But he knew that she had become an art-student, and that for a time she had prosecuted the activity in America. As she was merely a girl, and had thus not violated the military traditions of the Watlings in general, she had no doubt been allowed to follow her own inclinations in the matter. With what success she was busying herself as an artist, now, Appleby had never heard. But the fact would explain her taking up with the Lelys, who lived not far away.

'We've come to bag some tea,' Humphry Lely said cheerfully, as Appleby shook hands with the visitors. 'And we picked up Mary on the way. Mary was just walking for pleasure, and was getting tired of it. Kate and I' – Kate was Mrs Lely – 'were out on business.'

'Sketching *en plein air*?' Appleby asked.

'Something much more rewarding than that.'

'Simply drinking in inspiration,' the clerical Dr Folliott suggested humorously, 'from the meadows, groves, and streams.'

'Nothing of the kind. Pocketing the cash. And literally the cash. Fifty-pound notes. Think of that.'

'All in Humphry's bulging pockets now,' Mrs Lely said. 'Shall I, or will our little ones, ever see any of them again? I doubt it. Judith, I'm delighted to notice muffins. There's sense in muffins *en plein air*. And they sustain. May I unobtrusively secret a couple of them for the twins?'

'Whenever I hear,' Dr Folliott said, 'of unexpected brief affluence befalling a parishioner, I turn the conversation to the Mission Field. Or – more hopefully, it may be – to the state of our church's roof. To be dripped on during a sermon is a double affliction which everybody understands.'

Appleby reflected that Herbert Folliott, equally with Hoobin, was a perusing man. He spent most of his time, that was to say, with his nose happily in print. But whereas Hoobin's texts bore at least some distant relationship to the Queen's English, those favoured by Folliott were in Hebrew. Folliott was the odd sort of country clergyman who happens to be a theologian as well. All the more credit to him, surely, that on some afternoons he attended polite tea drinkings with their harmless chatter such as was now going on, and on others dodged in and out of cottages, helped old women to hang out their washing and children to recite with some approximation to accuracy even the more advanced of their multiplication tables.

'I hope,' Judith was saying to the vicar, 'that the bazaar went well?' This was simply Judith doing her stuff – as she always did. Equally with her husband, she no doubt judged it odd that institutions for public worship and the administering of sacraments should have to fund themselves out of cake and candy stalls. But she said the right things, which Appleby himself often culpably neglected to do. And Dr Folliott, although he presumably held the same persuasions much more strongly, always made the right replies.

'Thank you – yes,' he now said. 'Mary here was a tower of strength to me.'

'I blew up balloons,' Mary Watling said. 'Not with honest puff, but from a cylinder of some sort of gas. So they were real balloons, and floated on a string above the heads of the children who had given their pennies for them. Quite often they escaped, of course, and soared off into the air. It was rather like a psychological experiment. Some of the bereft children raged, some blubbered, some watched delighted and entranced, and others at once stumped off to mum or dad for the means to buy another balloon. Recorded on a sufficient scale to admit of significant statistical analysis, there might be quite a study in it after the Piaget fashion.'

Appleby glanced at Mary Watling with some interest. Her account of the children had been lively and first-hand; the bit about Piaget was the dutiful addition of a college-bred girl. That she had been very seriously an art student was perhaps questionable. Her American trip had probably been a matter of having a good time.

'And Mrs Carson at Garford was most generous,' Dr Folliott was saying, and at the same time he glanced at Judith with a faintly conspiratorial amusement. Judith, no doubt, had stumped up rather well, but was not to be complimented across her own alfresco tea-table. 'She sent several gallons of milk – really a wonderful idea – and also a sack of somewhat mysteriously special potatoes.'

Thus to qualify Cynthia Carson's potatoes was perhaps not quite the thing. But Appleby didn't think of this. Because he had been glancing at Mary Watling, he was aware of something slightly odd about her. At the mention of Mrs Carson at Garford she had perceptibly stiffened, and directed her gaze on her own toes. There was something perplexingly wary about this. But now Humphry Lely was speaking.

'It's at Garford,' he said, 'that Kate and I have been spoiling the Egyptians. You remember, John, the luncheon we had there? It led to my painting the chap's portrait – right in the heart of his own domain. I had it home for some days for a little hocussing, and then we shoved it in the van and delivered it this afternoon.'

'Is it a success?' Judith asked.

'I hardly know as to that. But I think perhaps not. In fact, the chap rather eluded me. But not in the financial sense. He did very promptly fork out.'

'Humphry,' Mrs Lely said, 'do tell.' This was a favourite exhortation on the part of Lely's wife. 'For it really was rather amusing.'

'It was rather awkward, in a way. The chap was a bit jumpy, for a start. Of course it's not unusual, that. Having yourself as a chum on your own wall does seem to be upsetting at times. But the point is that I expected him to write me out a cheque. It's what he'd said he'd do, as a matter of fact. But he just unlocked a drawer and a whopping great drawer it was – and counted me out the proper number of those fifty-pound notes. Made me thumb through them like a bank clerk, too, to make sure he'd got it just right. The drawer was absolutely stuffed with the things. Tight wads of them. It struck me they might be intended as an eccentric sort of present for that son of his back from America.'

'The son is really back?' Appleby asked in some surprise. 'Robin Carson?'

'Well, he didn't seem to be around. But I suppose so. At the last sitting Carson gave me he said he'd had a cable from the lad a day or two before saying that he was more or less on his way.'

'I see.' Appleby wondered whether he did see – or at least see anything relevant to his small Carson mystery. In his actual visual field, indeed, there was something to remark. At the first mention of the elusive Robin, Mary Watling had again acted in a rather odd fashion. She had stood up, murmured something to her hostess, and walked away down the nearest garden path. There was no hurry about it; every now and then, indeed, Mary paused as if to admire the efforts of Hoobin and Solo in one herbaceous border or another. It wasn't, on so informal an occasion, an unmannerly thing to do. Nevertheless, she had set a distance between herself and any further casual talk about the people at Garford House.

The Lelys departed, banknotes and all, taking Mary Watling along with them. Judith excused herself, explaining to the vicar that she had something baking in an oven: an ambiguous statement from which Dr Folliott didn't fail to extract a pleasantry.

'I shan't inquire,' he said, 'whether your concern is of a culinary or a ceramic order. Perhaps, after a fashion, it's both. Into your kiln has gone what will emerge as a succulent china fish, or even an enormous plum pudding, complete with sprigs of holly. But I forget how abstract your art has lately become, my dear.' Folliott had been a family friend for many years, and with Judith in particular enjoyed talking nonsense which would have merely perplexed most of his other parishioners.

'I very much hope it's my dinner,' Appleby said. 'But, talking of fish, come down to the pond, Herbert, and view Solo's latest. He becomes steadily more ambitious – and of course we are glad to see him taking an active interest in anything. He buys the monstrosities, and I pay the bills. His latest acquisition is a couple of telescope-fish.'

'Dear me! I fear I haven't heard of them.'

'They must be a product of Chinese ingenuity, I suppose. They look rather like mini-bull-dogs in a state of extreme terror. Their eyes almost pop out of their heads. Solo will gaze at them for an hour on end, without once remembering to drop asleep.'

'Telescope-fish sound highly disagreeable, so I am the happier to learn that they have some therapeutic virtue. By all means let us inspect them.'

So they walked down to Solo's pond and viewed the goldfish. They were numerous and varied, and it was clear that Solo's taste inclined to the grotesque.

'Yes,' Dr Folliott said presently. 'Yes, indeed. They appear to take some explaining, do they not? Where can possibly be any answer to the riddle they present? Perhaps, my dear John, the problem may be solved by reflecting on the doctrine of the Divine Abundance. God, you know, has to kill not merely time, but all eternity as well. So he calls into being absolutely everything he can think of. Even fish like mini-bulldogs. Yes – that must be it.'

'Perhaps so. But it makes God sound uncommonly like a Chinaman.' Appleby could say anything to Folliott. 'I was in China once, and stared at the Great Wall. I think I'd agree that only the Deity could have conceived that.'

'Indubitably. But Solo, now.' Dr Folliott had turned away from the fish pond, and Appleby realized at once from his tone that he had become serious. 'For some time I've had it in mind to have a word with Judith about your Solo. There's record of the boy's having been baptized – and in fact I can recall the occasion quite clearly. But, although he must be coming up to eighteen, I can't find that he has ever been confirmed. It's a real problem, John. But not, of course, unique. Rural society turns up no end of Solos. If one is in contact with them over a reasonable span of time, can they be deemed to have been adequately prepared or instructed for confirmation? I don't know that the whole bench of bishops has ever contrived to talk much sense about the problem. But Judith – who you will permit me to say is more of a churchwoman than you are a churchman, my dear fellow – may have a more useful opinion on this particular instance of the general puzzle. For it *is* a puzzle, wouldn't you say?'

'My own puzzle at the moment is those people at Garford.'

Appleby made this not very deft transition abruptly, since he was experiencing the common discomfort of agnostic persons when suddenly confronted with assumptions and convictions alien to them. And Dr Folliott understood this at once.

'Ah, yes,' he said. 'Garford. There are perplexities there, beyond a doubt. And not wholly remote from what we must call the Solo problem. Mrs Carson, so prodigal of potatoes and the products of vaccimulgence, is dotty in her own way.'

'I rather agree – although on a very slight acquaintance.' Appleby had taken a moment to nail 'vaccimulgence'. 'She's much taken up with their son – and in a commonplace and unremarkable manner. He did wonderfully at Harvard, and that sort of thing. It's on other subjects that she's rather odder. But there's just something – an elusive something – that I don't quite get hold of.'

'I don't exactly see, John, what you find positively perturbing – as I have a notion you do – about the Garford set-up. If indeed, one can speak about such a thing. Perplexities, as I've said. But look at any household steadily, and puzzles emerge.'

'It's the man more than the woman. We lunched with the Carsons a little time ago, and I didn't think much about them. But then their son came home, or started coming home, and some sort of hitch seems to have developed. It doesn't sound at all interesting. But the other day Carson turned up on me in rather an unaccountable fashion. What he had on his mind, he said, was just this of the boy's not arriving. But he had come over to tell me that we ourselves –

Judith and I – mustn't be worried about it. That struck me as moonshine. And the man himself was more worried than he confessed to being. That was quite in order: an Englishman keeping a stiff upper lip – that sort of thing. But I had a sense that a more complex piece of play-acting than that was going on. It keeps bothering me. And there's the further fact that Carson is either suddenly very hard up or – again – putting on a turn that way. I just don't, at the moment, make any clear sense of it.'

'Would a man who was very hard up keep a large drawer stuffed with fifty-pound notes?'

'Well, yes, he just might. It's a matter of scale, isn't it? If a man is hard up on what you might call a heroic scale, he may find it convenient to keep a mere few thousand pounds in the form of cash in hand.'

'Dear me! Of course that is so. How naive I am in money matters, John. But what about *pretending* to be hard up? It's an odd notion in itself.'

'Not necessarily in, say, a domestic context. For instance, one might so pretend by way of curbing one's wife's extravagance, or one's children's extravagance. But that isn't quite the puzzle here. Supposing that Carson, for some more obscure reason, *is* making such a pretence, why should he go out of his way to open a drawer stuffed with money under the very nose of an intelligent spectator? I can think, by the way, of one reason that *isn't* particularly obscure for getting together cash in a large way. One's business affairs are so embarrassed, and one's conduct of them has been so doubtful, that one is preparing to make oneself scarce with one's pockets full of pence. But in such a situation one certainly doesn't open that drawer on the pennies.'

For some paces Dr Folliott walked in silence. Perhaps he was digesting these curious considerations. Or perhaps – Appleby thought – he disapproved of this sort of anatomy of parishioners who at least sent large supplies of milk and potatoes to a kind of jumble sale. It was Appleby himself, after all, who had started this gossip about them. But it turned out that the vicar had only been preparing a relevant question.

'Just what is the evidence, John, that our friend is either hard up or pretending to be so?'

'It can only be described as something on the lips of the folk – which doesn't sound too impressive. But things have been happening – and they sound *obtrusive* things. A costly car and valuable pictures vanish more or less overnight. Or they do so unless I've been told a fairy-tale.'

'And it's the obtrusiveness that you judge significant?'

'Exactly that.' Appleby was impressed by Dr Folliott's rapid taking of this point. 'And it would seem to incline the scale fairly decisively on the side of pretence. But perhaps we can go a little further, although it's in a distinctly conjectural direction. Carson does need money. But he needs it for one purpose and is pretending it's for another.'

'My dear John – deep waters!'

'Yes, indeed. And I'm beginning to wonder whether the mysteriously missing son may not somehow be involved.'

'Robin – isn't that his name? The young man may have had to go into hiding because he has done something criminal or disgraceful, and a great deal of ready money has suddenly to be organized on his behalf – say to set him up in comfort in Timbuctoo.'

'Excellent, Herbert! You might be the man from Scotland Yard.'

'But, John, I am nothing of the kind. I am the clerk in holy orders here on the spot. And I don't doubt that I ought to be thinking no evil.'

Appleby supposed this to be, in a sense, a gentle rebuke. But he took it in good part.

'And no more have I any business to be meddling,' he said. 'A restless retired old fogy, am I not? Only I have a feeling, you see – although a confused one – that the thing may somehow drive on to a thoroughly sinister conclusion. Unless something is done about it, that is.'

'And that something you'd rather like to do yourself?'

'Well, yes, Herbert – I do confess to that. Am I wrong?'

For some paces Dr Folliott considered this question in a slightly disconcerting silence.

'We are old friends, are we not?' he then said.

'Yes, indeed.'

'And of Judith I am an older friend still. So I may be frank, John, and tell you how the thing strikes me. You are conceivably in some danger of barging in on a mare's nest. We have reviewed certain rather unaccountable circumstances, and it may well be true that what you call something thoroughly sinister is incubating in them. But, equally conceivably, it is innocent – and also private – matters that are alone involved. If you turned out to be intruding on nothing more than that, you'd feel, you know, rather an ass.'

'That's perfectly true, Herbert.' Appleby felt distinctly chastened. 'On the other hand' – and here Appleby rallied – 'if I washed my hands of the nonsense and something uncommonly bad did ensue, I'd feel I had shirked a responsibility, if only' – and Appleby added this humorously – 'as a JP, you know.'

'Very well. But why not have a word about it all with our friend Pride? He's a discreet man, is Tommy Pride. I suppose him to be not far off retirement himself. But meantime he has, I suppose, an active duty to keep an eye on possibly fishy goings-on in the county. Or his men have. I'd have a chat with Tommy, if I were you.'

'An excellent plan,' Appleby said. 'I'll carry it out as soon as I can get hold of him. Busy fellows, chief constables, these days. But I can rely on Tommy to lend an ear.'

Later that evening, Appleby reported to Judith on his encounter with the young man at the petrol-station.

'William Lockett,' he said, 'lives with his stepfather, the gardener over at Garford, and lends him a hand with the job. But now the forecourt employment is folding up on him – and just at a time he has decided that Garford is a sinking ship and he'd better get out of that too.'

'A sinking ship? Does that mean you take this William to be a bit of a rat?'

'Nothing of the sort, or I'd hardly be thinking about him. He's a little short of proper menial deference, perhaps' – Appleby was rather fond of routine ironies – 'but he strikes me as quite an alert lad with a noticing mind.'

Judith took a moment to consider this.

'John,' she asked, 'aren't you becoming rather obsessed with Garford and those Carsons?'

'Yes, I am. But just stick to William Lockett for a moment. It's my idea that we might take him on – of course in an explicitly temporary way – full-time. There's a good deal Hoobin and Solo will never get round to. All those saplings in the copse that have choked one another to death – and so long ago that you can snap them off like matches. Solo enjoys doing that. But of course they ought to be grubbed out, and the whole place given air. There would be a month's work for William Lockett at that alone.'

'Three weeks.' It was Judith who had the more accurate sense of the conduct of economic affairs at Long Dream. 'So why not?'

'Of course the young man will have to pass a kind of *viva voce* examination with Hoobin. I'll see to that, if William comes over to Dream. And Hoobin sounds not ill-disposed to the idea. Incidentally, William must be about ages with Solo, and might liven him up.'

'It might work the other way – Solo and your William sitting down together by that pool and adoring the finny tribe. But I quite agree to giving it a go. And now, John, be a bit clearer about why you have this man Carson on your mind.'

'The point is that I'm *not* clear. He perplexes me. I've been talking to Herbert Folliott about it, and Herbert has more or less told me to mind my own business. But I have an obstinate feeling that it *is* my own business – or what was my own business when I was *in* business.'

'You mean there's something criminal about it?'

'In a hazy way – yes. Or at least fishy. Listen. This Robin Carson cables that he's coming home, and then fails to turn up. His mother gets uneasy, but Carson himself asserts there's no real cause for alarm.'

'That's natural enough. He doesn't want to increase that silly woman's anxiety, so he denies his own misgivings about it.'

'It's not so simple as that. Carson *is* worried – which is fair enough. But he goes out of his way to ensure that the fact seeps through his assertions of unconcern. It's as if he wants observers to conclude that he has some very specific reason for being in great anxiety about his son. He's being, you may say, covertly emphatic about that. And also about something else: a sudden need for a lot of money. Herbert Folliott suggests that this precious Robin may have got into a serious scrape, and that a great deal of hard cash is required to get him out of it.'

'So that the father is conniving, perhaps, at his son's escaping from the law? It does sound as if it may be like that.' Judith Appleby paused for a moment. 'But, John, if it *is* that, I'm quite clear that you ought not to be sticking your oar in. Doing a bloodhound act on a man who's trying to get his son out of a mess! It just isn't on.'

'I suppose I need hardly say that I agree. Let Carl Carson get the better of my old chums the cops, and good luck to him. Only, you see, it's mayn't be like that. Not *quite* like that. Folliott may be in the target area, but the bull's eye may have eluded him. And whether one ought to interfere or not simply can't be decided until we know rather more than we do.'

11

On the following morning William Lockett turned up promptly on a bicycle. It wasn't clear what arrangement, if any, he had made for the stray motorist to be provided with petrol at what was presumably still his place of employment, and Appleby didn't inquire. Appleby acknowledged to himself that he was being a shade disingenuous over William, and that he wouldn't have discovered in himself an urgent need for an under-gardener if the young man didn't live where he did. But once a copper – he told himself – a copper for keeps. You find extra eyes and ears where you can.

'You must understand,' he said with some severity, 'that Mr Hoobin has been in charge here for many years, and that you must recommend yourself to him if you are to have a temporary job. Can you use a scythe?'

'One of *those* things?' William stared. 'Do you want me to cut my own legs off? Don't make me laugh.' William paused on this thought (which had been approximately Hoobin's as well). 'Sir,' he then added, presumably as a precautionary dollop of what Appleby had called menial deference.

'So far, so good, William. Mr Hoobin believes himself to be the last man left in the county who can command so much as a sickle. He also believes it to be dangerous to attempt to rouse his nephew Solo when the boy happens to have dropped off to sleep. Just remember that, and you may get along with Mr Hoobin agreeably enough. You'd better come and talk to him now.'

There followed upon this an interview in the potting shed that went quite well. William Lockett was hired. Appleby – as if treating him for the last time as a guest – then walked with him some way down the drive.

'And what about your stepfather?' he asked. 'Does he share your view that things are likely to go badly at Garford?'

'He hasn't got my sharpness, Dad hasn't.' As he offered this modest remark, William Lockett shot at Appleby a glance that his new employer found slightly disconcerting. It seemed to signal a persuasion that this elderly gent was a sucker for gossip about the neighbours. But that couldn't be helped.

'And has your sharpness,' Appleby asked, 'hit on anything new since I saw you yesterday?'

'It bloody well has. The whole dump gives me the willies, it does. And them Punters!'

'Those what – or who?'

'Him that's butler, and his wife that cooks and that. You must know Punter. Sir.'

'Ah, yes – I know the man you mean. But I've never passed the time of day with him.'

'Up to something, Punter is. Like the lot of them. Mad or bad: you can take your choice. I tell my dad he should pack up, even if it means going into a home for dotards. But he's attached to the place, having known better days there.'

'There's much to be said for attachment to a house and gardens.' Appleby produced this sententious remark while wondering how directly to go ahead. 'What were you going to say about something happening since yesterday?'

'It was like this, like. A hot day, wasn't it? And what with your flat tyre and all, I thought I'd quit those bloody pumps in time to get home for a pint of tea. That was how I came to see that Punter up to something. There's what's called a pergola at the bottom of the big garden – just where I skirt it to keep away from the house and be properly respectful to my betters. You know?'

'Well?' Appleby had given a brisk nod by way of indicating his awareness of this foolish social observance.

'It's a kind of covered walk, the pergola – with clematis and that. And at the end of it there's what they call an arbour – meaning a boarding-house for spiders and the like. But, this weather, Mrs Carson comes out regular before five o'clock, and sits in the thing with a bit of knitting – for all the world like an honest woman that has to keep the kids in socks. But this was a bit before that time, and what I saw was Punter.'

'Ah.'

'Coming along under the pergola, he was. Like a guilty thing.'

'Do you mean that he was approaching this arbour in a stealthy manner?'

'Just that. Sir. The old girl hadn't arrived yet – but she might have, if she'd been a bit early. So here was this Punter, peering ahead and looking about him. Naturally like, I took cover.'

'You constituted yourself an observer of this peculiar behaviour?'

'Just that. The bastard was up to something, wasn't he? He had a newspaper under his arm.'

'Did that strike you as sinister?'

'It was what he did with it, mate. Sir. He stopped and unfolded it and turned it back on a page that seemed to take his fancy. Then he crumpled it just a bit, and left it on the little wooden table in there – just as if it had been left careless like by my dad when he'd been in clearing up after the spiders. Then he went back to the house – as cautious as a cat.'

'But you continued to observe?'

'I didn't hurry.'

'Quite so, William. And was your patience rewarded by some further sensation?'

'It was. Bang on time, out came Mrs C knitting and all. The programme would continue then minutes later with Punter's wife bringing her out a cup of tea. But it didn't happen that way this time. Presently Mrs C spotted the newspaper, as she couldn't help but do. Then she picked it up and stared at it like the idle bitch she is. Beg your pardon. And the next moment or thereabout she was letting out a screech it might be like a tortured owl.'

'A tortured owl?' Appleby repeated doubtfully. He found this conception both unfamiliar and displeasing. 'Mrs Carson had come on something by which she was extremely alarmed?'

'You're telling me. Scared, it might be, out of her knickers. Then she jumped up and bolted for the house, still hollering.'

'Taking the newspaper with her?'

'That and waving it.'

'I'd rather she'd dropped it. You'd have had no means, I suppose, of retrieving it?'

'Of course not. She was into the house with it, and that was that.'

'Can you tell what newspaper it was?'

'That I can not. I just wasn't that near. Not to speak of my nose being in a cobweb.'

'Do you know what papers are taken regularly at Garford?'

'No clue, mate. Sir. Mrs Rumble – her at the post-office – she'd know.'

Appleby accepted this point in silence. His situation was now slightly awkward, since this little interview hadn't at all developed on that level of harmless gossip. William Lockett, however, took this changed state of affairs in his stride.

'You wouldn't be from the papers yourself?' he asked.

'Certainly not.'

'There's money, they say, in queer stories about the high-ups.'

'I don't know that the Carsons can be called high-ups. And there's no money around, William. Put that right out of your head. As for where I'm from, as you put it, it's my guess you know perfectly well. There's no hiding under bushels in rural society.'

'Scotland Yard, my dad says. Only, as you're getting on now, I thought you might be with a paper. A lot seem to end that way.' William said this on a note of disappointment.

'What you've got in your head, William, is probably something called cheque-book journalism. It's not on.'

'But dad says you ran the place. That right?'

'Scotland Yard? Yes, I ran it.'

'And having another go at that-like now?' William's eyes had rounded on Appleby. William wasn't at all dull. 'Christ!' he added, and paused for thought. 'Would it be Carson himself you're after? He's no better than his bloody butler, if you ask me.'

'Never mind whom I'm after. Just keep your eyes open – and your ears too, for that matter. But your mouth shut.'

'That's okay by me.'

'Then off you go.'

'Sir,' William Lockett said – and saw that Appleby had nodded towards his bicycle. So he mounted it and departed.

When Appleby returned to the house he gave a faithful account of this interview to his wife, and found that he had to encounter some displeasure.

'You're incorrigible,' Judith said. 'A sniff of crime, and you're like a bee going after honey. Or perhaps it's like a beetle after dung.'

'When I ought just to sit in the garden and do the crossword in *The Times.*'

'No, but seriously, John. You've got hold of this young man on false pretences, and are making a spy and an informer of him.'

'Seriously, then, by all means. It's quite evident that there's some mischief going on at Garford – but just what, I can't make out. It may be no more than some commonplace rascality I'd be an ass to tangle with. I give you that. But it may well be something much more sinister: outright skulduggery that ought to be put a stop to. And as for young Lockett, he won't come to any harm.'

'You're encouraging him to go peeping behind the gooseberry bushes instead of earning an honest living. That's harm.'

Judith, perhaps, was only half in earnest. Even so, she had a point. Appleby conscientiously endeavoured to persuade himself that he regretted the mysterious affair at Garford as having come his way. But it had. And there was nothing for it but to clear the thing up.

12

So on the following morning Appleby took his next step: a telephone call to the regional police headquarters and the making of an appointment with the Chief Constable at twelve noon. Tommy Pride was unlikely ever to have heard of Carl Carson. But he was the man who could quickly cause to be turned up a certain amount of peripheral information which Appleby felt increasingly anxious to acquire. Appleby had a high regard for Tommy's sagacity, as well as for the discretion that commended him to Dr Folliott. But what he chiefly esteemed, perhaps, was the strength of the machine on which the Chief Constable could press the buttons. It wasn't quite the machine which Appleby himself had ended up with – and, indeed, Appleby had at times made fun of what he called the Dogberry element in the forces under Tommy's command. But Tommy himself, although inclined to dissimulate any expertness in the techniques of criminal investigation, was no Dogberry, let alone a Verges. He was uncommonly astute. He was also a very busy man, which made all the more remarkable the effect of large leisure with which he greeted Appleby – who was, of course, an old friend.

'Things not too good in London, John,' he said cheerfully, 'since they handed you your cards. Large-scale robbery every thirty-six minutes, isn't it, right round the clock? Or something like that. Never good at holding figures in my head.'

'They have problems there, without a doubt.'

'Go back and lend a hand, eh? Who was that chappie the Wogs called back from the plough?'

'Cincinnatus, I believe.'

'That's it. Did the job, and then returned to the farm. Recommend it to you. Make a break from Judith's roses.' That much of Appleby's time had to be devoted to horticultural effort was a perennial joke with the Chief Constable. 'Or, failing that, what about lunch? I can do you a quiet glass of sherry here, and then we could run over to Burford or Woodstock.'

'I won't say no to the sherry, Tommy, but then I must get back home. I have my eye on a crime. Or on a crime *in posse*, as Cincinnatus' fellow Wogs used to say.'

'God bless my soul! And you've come to tell me about it? Go right ahead.'

And Appleby went ahead.

'It's about some people called Carson,' he said. 'They're tolerably near neighbours of mine. The man has concerns in the City, and he and his wife have a son called Robin, who seems to have spent most of his young life in the States. But now he's come home on a visit. Or that was the idea. Only he seems to have got lost on the way.'

'I see – but it doesn't sound terribly serious so far.' The Chief Constable was hospitably producing sherry from a cupboard. 'On what sort of scale is neighbour Carson, City-wise?'

'Moderately substantial, I imagine. A Rolls-Royce in the shed, and pictures by approved masters on the walls. Or that until just lately. Now they've got lost just like Robin.'

'What the Capital Transfer chappies call a marked change in one's standard of living, would you say?'

'It may stretch to that. What appears to me to be happening is that the fellow is going for sudden liquidity like mad. I believe that's the expression. Collecting simple and straightforward cash in a big way.'

'Elementary, my dear John. Your friend is in trouble on the markets, and is preparing to do a bunk. Do I divine that you don't greatly care for him? He won't be troubling you for long. Dallas, or some such place, is his natural home. And he's on his way. May even take his wife. I suppose there is a wife?'

'Yes – and she's a bit dotty. It's true that I don't greatly take to Carson. But I'm not sure he isn't to be sympathized with – and even given some cautious support.'

'By the police, you mean?' Pride had sat back in his chair. 'I'm to see to it in a quiet way that nobody quarrels with his passport, or holds him on some convenient trumped-up affair about his dog licence? Anything to oblige an old chum, of course.'

'It's not quite that.' Appleby paused to let the Chief Constable's innocent pleasure in his own sense of fun subside. And when he did speak, it was with care. 'There's a good deal that doesn't fit in with what I'm going to suggest. There's a butler who behaves in a mysterious way, and a nice girl – also a neighbour – whose conduct is equally odd whenever the name of the elusive Robin turns up. But what *does* fit in are certain peculiar undercurrents in the bearing of Carson himself. His wife is worried about Robin's non-appearance, but he declares he is not. But he *is* worried, all the same. I must say at once that there's a kind of sub-text to his professions that I just sense without managing to get the hang of. But the main *clou* in the whole affair, I'm coming to think I *have* got hold of. Robin's failure to turn up in the old home hasn't been a matter of Robin's own free will. It's my hunch that the young man has been kidnapped *en route*; that his father has been intimidated into not calling in the police; and that all the money being hastily got together is required to ransom him while keeping the whole thing dark. It's because of that possibility, Tommy, that I've turned up on you. Nothing's more delicate – is it? – police-wise than just that situation.'

'True enough.' Pride spoke very quietly this time. 'But, John, I wonder whether you ought to have come to me before going to Carson himself? Don't misunderstand me. I simply mean that perhaps you should have tried him out with what you believe to be the truth. And, if he admitted it, put to him the case for coming to me himself. Or going to the local copper, for that matter. That would have seen it on my desk – I can assure you – in no time at all.'

'I can still do that: tackle Carson, I mean. But after something only you can do. Press the buttons, Tommy.'

'Meaning just what?'

'Check up, over the past fortnight, on anything that looks like a possible kidnapping affair and that hasn't been sorted out. The thing mayn't have happened at all, and I may be quite wrong. Or it may have happened efficiently and without leaving a trace. Or somebody may have seen, and reported, just something. And it's not a matter of every file in the country. We needn't bother with the Orkneys and Shetlands.'

'Or the Outer Hebrides, I suppose.' The Chief Constable had reached for a telephone. 'Computer boffins forward – eh, John? Can't say I understand their contraptions. Much like the ancient johnnies consulting oracles. Go to sleep inside the skin of a dead sheep, and the correct dream bobs up on you.' Tommy Pride, who seemed to favour somewhat cloudy analogies from classical antiquity, dialled a number. 'But at least the boffins handle their hardware briskly. I'll sift through what they turn up myself, and get in touch with you either late this afternoon or early tomorrow.'

'I'll be most grateful to you. And so – if things go well as a result of our mucking in – may those wretched Carsons be in the end.' Appleby got up to go. 'But that puts one further thing in my head. I've been favoured with an odd yarn – reliable, I think, although perhaps a little spiced up in the telling – about something that happened to Mrs Carson only yesterday. She picked up a newspaper in rather mysterious circumstances, and was much upset by something she read in it. It's an episode I can't quite fit into the jigsaw, if jigsaw there be. But you might have somebody rake through the papers over, say, the past fortnight in search of anything likely to alarm a nervous lady with kidnapping or wayside violence or the like stirring in her head.'

'At least that's an easy one.' The Chief Constable made a note. 'Leaving no stone unturned is quite our sort of thing.'

When he got home Appleby was informed that a gentleman had called on what he declared to be urgent business. Told that Sir John was out but expected back shortly, he had said he would wait. The Appleby's home-help had disapproved of this – which hadn't even come in the form of a suggestion or request. But it hadn't occurred to her to require the caller's name, and she had simply shown him, if with some misgiving, into the breakfast-room. He was there now.

Appleby didn't care for anonymous visitors. They commonly turned out to want to sell something. If Judith hadn't happened to be on a shopping expedition, she'd have bowed this intrusive person out promptly enough. It was with a sense, therefore, of slight irritation that Appleby now made his way to the breakfast-room. What he found there was a young man comfortably disposed in an armchair. The young man got to his feet without haste.

'Sir John Appleby?' he asked. 'I must introduce myself. My name is Peter Pluckworthy.'

'How do you do?' Appleby was not really much concerned about Mr Pluckworthy's health. 'Can I help you in any way?'

Modern English usage has done a good job on this locution, since on its surface it is blameless and even benevolent, while a little lower down being as chilly as you please.

Pluckworthy seemed to receive it as a cordial expression of concern.

'I'm Carl's secretary,' he said engagingly.

'Carl?'

'Carl Carson. I call him Carl because I'm also, you might say, a friend of the family.'

'Then you know Robin?'

This question, crisply put, seemed slightly to disconcert Mr Pluckworthy. He answered, however, readily enough.

'Well, no – I've never met Robin Carson. He lives, you see, mostly in America. But it's about him, as it happens, Sir John, that I've really come to see you.'

'You surprise me. But explain yourself.'

'I know it must seem odd – and odder when I say that I'm acting off my own bat. It's from anxiety about Cynthia – Mrs Carson, that is – that I've ventured to drop in. She's terribly worried, and I'm very fond of her.'

'I am sorry the lady should be distressed, and I shall be most grateful to hear there is anything I can do about it. Just what?'

'It does take a little explaining, Sir John, and I hope you will bear with me.' Pluckworthy appeared to be a young man as confident of his own good manners as of his own sharp wits. 'I think you already know that Mrs Carson is very worried about what she feels to be an inexplicable delay in her son's turning up at Garford. We have to suppose he has been on his way for quite some time to pay a visit to his parents. But for days there has been no sign of him, or word from him either. So Cynthia's anxiety is understandable. Carl is much less worried. Perhaps he knows a little more about young men.'

Pluckworthy paused on this, as if expecting Appleby to produce some appropriate observation. But this didn't happen, and he continued.

'I hate to say it, but in some ways Cynthia isn't always quite clear in her head. Carl has been a little embarrassed by some of her reactions to the situation.'

'Mr Carson called on me to say something of the kind. I thought it slightly odd – as I am still inclined to judge your own call now, Mr Pluckworthy.'

'I'm so sorry. Perhaps I'm not a good hand at explaining myself.' Pluckworthy produced what he would probably have described as a wry smile. 'I know that Cynthia rang up Lady Appleby with some notion of enlisting your help in finding Robin. I hope you regarded it as excusable. Of course she knows of your former high rank in the police. And her anxieties are reasonable too in a way. After all, you know, she had a phone call from Robin at Heathrow – and after that there has been this silence. It *is* a little worrying.'

'I am inclined, Mr Pluckworthy, to regard it as a little more than that. But I still don't know what you expect me to do.'

'Nothing.'

'I beg your pardon?'

'I've come to ask you to do nothing.' For a moment Pluckworthy's readiness seemed to desert him. He might have been hunting about for words. And it was somewhat tartly (and more than somewhat disingenuously) that Appleby took him up.

'My dear young man, why should you suppose that I contemplate interfering in the matter? And how could I do it if I did?'

'Come, Sir John. A word from you would set the entire police force of the county hunting for this wretched young man. Or nation-wide, for that matter.'

'I fear, Mr Pluckworthy, that you overestimate the influence of a retired metropolitan man. But the merits of what you touch on are another matter. Now that you have put it in my head, I think I might well have a word with the Chief Constable. His men probably enjoy practice in setting up road-blocks and searching empty garages – and even dredging canals and diving into ponds.'

'It might be absolutely fatal!' Pluckworthy had sprung to his feet, apparently in uncontrollable agitation. Then he checked himself and sat down again. 'The point is that I think it possible that Mrs Carson may make another appeal to you – and at a pitch you might find it difficult to resist. It seems – I had a telephone call from Carl only this morning – that she has come on some alarmist and sensational rubbish in a newspaper. About some sort of fracas just off a motorway, I gather. And she has taken it into her head that Robin must have been mixed up in it. That he has been robbed and killed and heaven knows what.'

'Have you any positive proof, Mr Pluckworthy, that Mrs Carson's persuasion is unjustified?'

'Unjustified?' It was clearly for the sake of gaining time that Pluckworthy echoed this word. He was momentarily at a loss how to reply. But then he recovered himself. 'But it's such obvious nonsense!' he exclaimed. 'Why should anyone fall on this young man – virtually a stranger in England – and rob him or kidnap him or beat him up or whatever?'

'The word of most weight there, I imagine, is "kidnap". Isn't Robin Carson's father a very wealthy man?'

Pluckworthy's response to this question was to make an odd groping gesture which for a moment had Appleby baffled. Then he saw that his visitor was reaching for an umbrella which he had deposited on the carpet beside him. He was being prompted, in fact, to bolt from the room. But again – if very uncertainly – he rallied.

'Well, yes,' he said, 'I suppose it's a rational suspicion. But...'

'But if this distressed lady comes to me with what you now agree to be a rational fear for the safety of her son, you want me to decline to do anything about it? I am to dismiss her as a muddle-headed person? Or do I mistake you, Mr Pluckworthy?'

This sudden broadside brought the young man to his feet again – and looking rather wildly round the room as if to remind himself where he would find the door.

'It's all just too difficult!' he cried. 'I've made a mess of it. I oughtn't to have come. I'm sorry – really frightfully sorry, Sir John. But I do beg of you – really beg of you – to hold your hand so far as the police are concerned. It would be disastrous. Please believe me. Goodbye!'

And with this Carl Carson's secretary took himself off, seemingly in blind disarray. But at least he had taken his umbrella with him, and at least he was quickly in command of his car. Within a minute the sound of an engine was diminishing down the drive.

'Whoever was that?' Judith asked. 'He came charging through the hall, and almost knocked this shopping-basket out of my hand.'

'A young gentleman called Pluckworthy, who describes himself as Carson's secretary, and a family friend.'

'And what was he doing here?'

'You saw what he was doing. I believe it's called creating.'

'Mounting a scene?'

'It would perhaps be injudicious to say more than that he has a distinct stage sense. But so many people have, that the fact isn't notable in itself. He said he'd come to see me off his own bat – which rather makes me think he hadn't. In fact, I take him to be an emissary of his employer. And the picture now is this. The unfortunate Mrs Carson has had another shock about her Robin. That, I know to be true. I also know that it was administered, as one may put it, in a covert way by the Carson butler, Punter. Just why, heaven knows. But the idea of Messrs Carson and Pluckworthy seems to be that the lady is due to make a fuss about it all on a larger scale than before.'

'Than on the occasion, you mean, of her ringing me up to enlist your help?'

'Just that. And why not? Almost anyone would say it was high time to investigate this entire Robin business.' Appleby suddenly laughed softly. 'As I happen to be doing myself in a quiet way. I've set Tommy Pride working.'

'Did you tell this Pluckworthy person about that?'

'No I didn't. In perplexed situations there is much to be said for reticence. And what is chiefly perplexing – if perhaps only superficially so – is that Carson and Pluckworthy feel that the lady ought to be discouraged. And that I ought to be as well. You might say they're all for taking it lying down. Each seems to go out of his way to obtrude – repeat, obtrude – both confidence that the whole thing is nonsense, and alarm and funk about it. There seems to be a contradiction in that. But the main pivot of the thing looks like being wide open.'

'Can pivots be wide open, John?'

'Don't quibble. I mean that the wretched Robin Carson has been waylaid and kidnapped when making for the sanctity of the family home. He's being held to ransom, in fact, and Carson and his henchman are trying – although in a confused way – to keep the fact from the police while Carson hastily scrambles together the money required to ransom the boy. I've put that – but with a certain misgiving, I'm bound to say – to Tommy, and it's my hope that the fact will presently establish itself beyond doubt.'

'There will have been threats about Robin's safety, and even about his life?'

'There have been, or there will be. Mrs Carson may receive one of her son's ears through the post. That sort of thing.'

'John, you take on a terrible responsibility in having anything to do with it.'

'That's obvious. It's equally obvious that I have to behave rationally about it. Villains have to be caught, you know, even at the cost of an enhanced risk to third persons. But there's more to it than that. Carson on his own has no means of setting a trap for the criminals. Given a fair chance, the police have. And I myself am just waiting for Tommy to turn up a little more evidence before I tackle Carson himself and try to persuade him to co-operate.'

'You mean you want him to seem to be caving in and paying up, while really...'

'Just that. It takes nerve. Whether Carson has the nerve, or his young whipper-snapper has the nerve, of course I just don't know.'

'So meanwhile?'

'We have some tea, and wait for a telephone call from Tommy. Patience, Judith, and shuffle the cards.'

117

13

It has to be recorded of Sir John Appleby that at this point he was confident of having penetrated at least to the essentials of the Robin Carson mystery. He hadn't, of course, kept his conclusion to himself. He had mentioned it to his wife as a matter of course, and briefly expounded it to Tommy Pride as a matter of duty. Robin had been kidnapped on the last stage of his journey to Garford. He was being held for ransom now: a fact known to his father, though not with any precision to his mother. Carl Carson was hard at work getting the money together. It must be a very large sum that was being demanded, since Carson, clearly a wealthy man, was being so hard put to it. Appleby didn't greatly care for Carson; obscurely, he felt he hadn't quite got the hang of the man; but he would have been ashamed of himself if he hadn't felt sympathy with the father's plight. And the fellow had a downright silly wife, who was unlikely to be of much support to him. If William Lockett's story was to be trusted, the woman had now got near to the truth of the matter. Perhaps it would turn out that it was she, after all, who had the guts or the good judgement to go to the police.

Appleby found himself pausing on young Lockett's story, and felt that he saw further illumination in it. One snag in the path of the kidnap theory was the difficulty of seeing how the kidnappers had been aware in advance of Robin Carson's movements. Punter could now be viewed as the answer to that one. The butler was a crook and a spy, and had got hold of the essential facts through his employer and – more probably – his employer's wife. He had heard about that cable; and, with everything down to a vital hour or half hour, he had heard about that telephone call from Heathrow too. His covert planting of that newspaper in Mrs Carson's way explained itself as well. What she had there read had sharpened her fears about Robin; had, in fact, got them almost in the target area; had thus, no doubt, increased the pressure upon Carson himself.

All this clarity (as the retired Commissioner of Metropolitan Police saw it) at least defined the problem. But it didn't immediately help to a solution, if that solution was to be conceived of as primarily the rescuing of Robin Carson from his captors. Nothing is so dangerous, so ruthless, as a kidnapper or gang of kidnappers under threat of being cornered. Once the possibility of extortion vanishes, it is a matter – one may say – of cut and run, and the cutting may conceivably include an inconvenient captive's throat.

So what could be done – either with Carl Carson's concurrence or without it? Appleby's mind went to work on the problem in a professional way. Punter offered some hope. With just a shade more of evidence to connect Punter with the crime, it might be possible to take him in and intimidate or bribe him into grassing on his pals. Achieve that, and the hide-out where they were guarding their prisoner could be located, ringed, and closed in on. Ten to one, they'd then surrender. Presumably they, too, were professionals, unlikely to panic to the extent of cutting throats to no good purpose.

Appleby had got as far as this in his cogitations when he was called to the telephone. It was Tommy Pride.

'John? Good! Tommy here. No problem.'

'I don't believe that for a moment.'

'Don't you? You may be right. I just mean that what you wanted has turned up straight out of the hat. That newspaper para, for a start. In most of the rags in one form or another, just a week ago. But it's no more than a garbled version of something it turns out my neighbours are working on now.'

'Your neighbours, Tommy?'

'The cops in the next county. Of course, info on it has come in here, but I didn't know about it. Not everything is brought to me.'

'Heaven forbid.'

'Quite so. Well, it was conceivably your kidnap, although a precious rum specimen. One-man show, for a start. Did you ever hear of such a thing as that, John?'

'Often enough. Dad snatching a kid from mum, or mum from dad, and bolting to Australia or wherever.'

'I don't call that a kidnap. I call it mere family despair and misery.' The Chief Constable said this with a sudden sobriety that was almost a rebuke. 'Not that I go along with the way our people tend to shy away from what they call domestic disputes. I tell my chaps the Queen's peace has to be maintained, even if the brawl is between husband and wife in the back yard.'

'Physical violence being the crux, wouldn't you say? But get on with what you've been kind enough to turn up. The one-man kidnap.'

'It happened at dusk, just off the M4 and near Heathrow. Some little chappie was tootling along in his Mini when he came on a roadside rumpus. He stopped to watch it.'

'And just what did he see?'

'I gather his first observation was made while he was still on the move. There was another car ahead of him: perhaps, he says, a couple of hundred yards ahead. And there was a chap at the roadside, flagging it down.'

'Hitch-hiker?'

'Just a moment, John.' There was a brief pause during which the Chief Constable might have been consulting a note. 'Yes, here it is. The chappie thinks definitely not. More like somebody with a breakdown wanting a message taken to the nearest garage or any AA man.'

'Your chappie sounds to be one who prides himself on precise observations. Well?'

'So the car in front obligingly stopped, and there was a bit of a palaver. Then, just as this opportune witness was almost up on it, the really rum thing happened. In the halted car there was only a single young man. And what did he do? Jumped out – and in a moment what was going on was a bloody battle. Our man drew to a halt, sat – a bit nervously, I imagine – in his own car, and just watched the fray. It lasted no time. The man who'd done the flagging down broke clear, whipped out a gun, forced the young man back to his wheel at the point of it, jumped in beside him, and made him drive off at speed. Would you call that a kidnap?'

'Most definitely. And, as you remark, a pretty rum one at that. Economical, one might say. Does the story continue, Tommy?'

'Not very far. Of course the Mini man did nothing about it in the way of trying to interfere. It was all over too quickly, no doubt – and I don't know that I'd blame him for a little hanging back. He did find the nearest telephone, and ring the police.'

'Good mark.'

'Yes, and he earns another. He managed to memorize the registration number of the car.'

'And it has been traced?'

'Apparently so – but only this very morning. Parked at Heathrow.'

'Long term?'

'No. I don't think one can do that without contacting somebody. Just one of the multi-storey places. Not a bad hidey-hole for a week or so.'

'Has the car's provenance been traced yet?'

'Yes, it has. They've been uncommonly prompt. It's a self-drive car, and was hired – there at the airport – only about an hour before the kidnap happened. The hirer gave his name as Carson, and paid in cash.'

'In cash?' Appleby took this up at once. 'A bit unusual, surely. Those deals are generally done on a credit-card basis.'

'That's certainly so, but I suppose they don't mind if the money put down is big enough. What do you think of the whole picture, John?'

'I'm out of touch with these affairs, Tommy, but this one sounds a bit atypical. I suppose the chap in the Mini is to be relied on?'

'Another moment, John.' There was a short rustle of papers, and then the Chief Constable spoke again. 'Yes, they have something on that. Unexceptionable character, it says.'

'And there were some objective signs of a struggle?'

'Blood, it seems. The chap can't have drawn his gun straight off.'

'Odd. And this Robin Carson sounds to be quite a lad. Tumbling to the situation, jumping out of his car, and having a go with his fists. It almost seems to me…'

But at this moment Appleby was checked by a low buzzing on the line, and then the Chief Constable spoke again.

'Just hold on a minute – will you, John? That's the intercom I have to answer pronto.' This time, the pause was much longer. Then Pride was speaking again – decidedly on a new note. 'Hell's bells and bloody bodkins!' he exclaimed.

'My dear Tommy, whatever…?'

'Your confounded Mrs Carson, John. On the blower to my people here, and sounding, apparently, clean off her head.'

'She's a lady who does, at times, appear to be a little on the eccentric side. What's she rampaging about?'

'About her husband, your blasted neighbour.' The Chief Constable was plainly much rattled. 'She says he has disappeared.'

It must be admitted that Sir John Appleby, although he refrained from emulating the Chief Constable in point of bizarre ejaculation, failed to take this information entirely in his stride. There was a perceptible pause before he asked a question.

'Since when?'

'Yesterday afternoon.'

'That's not yet twenty-four hours ago – which isn't all that out of the way. There are married men – and, no doubt, married women – who are a bit casual about their coming and going. It's a reprehensible habit, as being sure to occasion anxiety. But Carson may be like that. I don't think of him as likely to be a very thoughtful person.'

'I gather they put that notion to his wife as tactfully as they could. She denied it flat. She said that Carl was very careful about intimating the probable length of his absences. His staying away for a night, without any word about it, she declares to be quite unexampled.'

'She seems at least to have been articulate. Do you gather she ran to any particulars?'

'Carson drove away in her car, taking a couple of suitcases.'

'Dear me! They must have required a little explaining.'

'Apparently he explained them to his butler. He said he was taking a lot of his winter clothes – overcoats and the like, one imagines – to the dry-cleaner. It sounds a bit odd. Do you think the fellow is levanting? You know what I mean. Doing a bunk from his creditors.'

'I'd say he's well within the category of persons about whom one might have such a thought. I've even had him more or less explicitly in my mind that way. But it doesn't – does it? – quite fit within the present context.'

'John, I've just thought of quite a fresh possibility. Mrs Carson sounds a thoroughly trying woman. Robin hasn't turned up simply because he has some sort of rendezvous with his father. They plan to bolt together just as soon as dad can collect enough money. As he has now done. What do you say to that?'

'Words simply fail me, Tommy.' It was true that this extraordinary suggestion had almost taken Appleby's breath away. 'I suggest we swap this telephone chat for deeds. Have a rendezvous of our own *chez* Carson in, say, an hour's time. The arrival of top brass might brace the lady, and get something useful out of her.'

'I agree to that.'

'Good. Incidentally, I'll probably bring a friend with me.'

'A friend, John?'

But Appleby had put down the receiver.

14

Appleby made a telephone call, and then drove over to Garford. On the way, he found himself giving some thought to Tommy Pride's notable suggestion. It can't be said that he entertained it. But he found it stimulating, all the same.

The notion of the Carsons, father and son, as being jointly engaged in financial and other dispositions making possible a simultaneous flight from the tiresomely dotty Cynthia Carson mightn't stand up to scrutiny, yet it held a certain attractiveness for the speculative mind. Eccentric behaviour is always in some degree infectious. History affords numerous examples of irrational beliefs and senseless conduct spreading from one group or community to another. The same mechanisms are frequently to be observed in domestic contexts, notably in the growth of what psychiatrists call *foli à deux*. The disorder, Appleby understood, most frequently afflicted sisters, or husband and wife. He wondered whether it ever got going on father and son.

But now a more relevant thought came to Appleby. A novel view – such as this of Tommy's – of some perplexing situation has a kind of magnetic force in it. One begins to see how many already established circumstances peripheral to the core of the thing can be locked into it in one way or another. But this is always liable to be a mere sporting with red herrings. When something new of an evidential character turns up, one's first job is not to slot it into an existing picture but to consider it with an absolutely open mind. There had been, for example, William Lockett's story of the sinister behaviour of Punter, the Carsons' butler, when in that covert way he had brought to Mrs Carson's notice a newspaper account which now looked as if it might have been of Robin Carson's kidnap. Appleby saw how he had himself shoved this into his existing jigsaw. Punter belonged to the conjectured gang of kidnappers, or at least was in their pay. His action had contrived further to destabilize Cynthia Carson, thereby enhancing her husband's desperation in face of his predicament and serving as a step in forcing him to pay up.

But this was not the right way in which to regard the Punter incident. Appleby saw no present reason to begin to doubt that Robin had been kidnapped and was being held to ransom. He also saw no reason to doubt that the young man's father had decided to knuckle under to the threat, and purchase his son's liberty. And although Carl Carson appeared to him a far from amiable or trustworthy character, and although his own entire professional career inclined him to the view that the man's behaviour was injudicious and even technically illegal, he by no means felt that he was to be censured outright. It was an agonizing situation, and he ought himself to act with the utmost caution and be sparing of speech about it. Moreover, whatever were his views, he ought to be chary of feeling that he was dealing with established fact. In considering Punter's role in the current mystery he ought to remember that. In one fashion or another, he might have got Punter entirely wrong.

It was Punter who opened the door when he rang the bell at Garford House. Punter failed to produce anything that could be called a welcoming smile. But perhaps, Appleby thought, the man judged anything of the kind to be unbecoming in a butler except when a caller happened to be an established friend of the family. Punter's expression might have been described as impassive, had it not contrived to hint at one and the same time a conventional respect and the suspicion with which one regards a caller who has put up an unconvincing story of having come to do something about the drains.

'Is Mrs Carson at home?' Appleby asked.

'Mrs Carson is indisposed, sir. She regrets that she is not receiving.'

This was very august. Appleby tried again.

'Mr Carson, perhaps?'

'Mr Carson was called away on business yesterday afternoon.' Punter paused on this. 'We are given to understand,' he then added in a wooden manner.

'I see. I think I will ask you to take my card to Mrs Carson, and say that I hope to speak to her for a few minutes. And add that two other callers are likely to turn up within the next quarter of an hour. Mr Lely, whom, I think, you know, and the Chief Constable of the county.' Appleby contrived an august pause of his own. 'The Chief Constable and I are engaged on an inquiry in which Mrs Carson is likely to be of help to us. It is very probable that you will have to answer some questions yourself.'

If the butler was perturbed by these intimations he concealed the fact. Ushering Appleby into the hall with a solemn bow, he received on a salver the scrap of pasteboard offered to him, and withdrew into the recesses of the house. Appleby glanced about him – perhaps with the notion of detecting evidences of the sudden exigency that had been responsible for the abrupt spiriting away of the Romneys, the Reynoldses, and the Rolls-Royce. But the hall was as he remembered it, containing nothing more portable than a couple of life-size marble statues in niches: Victorian assertions of the unflawed propriety of female nudity when done in something sufficiently impenetrable and chilly white. Appleby recalled his wife as having shuddered at these as she passed them on the occasion of the Carsons' luncheon party.

Punter returned. He preserved his formal manner. But it was now combined, if not with a shifty, at least with a wary glance. He had certainly been up to no good on that garden occasion, and perhaps he was coming to suspect that he had somehow been detected in it. Appleby remembered forming an unfavourable impression of the man when he first set eyes on him. He had known himself to do just that of persons who had subsequently proved to be totally blameless. He wondered, all the same, whether this upper-servant business was in any permanent way Punter's authentic walk of life.

'If you will come this way, Sir John.' Punter uttered this invitation, or command, with all the consequence of a court chamberlain deciding to accord the *grande entrée* to a minor nobleman not quite deserving it. But halfway down a corridor he came to a halt and turned to Appleby. 'I wonder, sir,' he said, 'whether I might have your permission to offer an observation?'

'My good man, if you have anything to say, by all means out with it.' It was probably many years since Appleby had addressed anybody as 'my good man', and he wouldn't have done so now had he not been feeling a mounting irritation with Punter. The man was overacting a part in a positively clumsy way. He wasn't too bright, was Punter. If he was a crook, he was a small-time one. And he seemed quite unoffended by Appleby's lapse.

'I am merely moved to warn you, Sir John, that you will find Mrs Carson in a distraught condition. She has been worried for some time by the failure of Mr Robin Carson to visit us at Garford. It would appear…'

'Yes, I know about that, Mr Punter. Anything else?'

'And now Mr Carson himself. She is worried about him too.'

'Quite so. Would you say those worries were justified?' It was with a calculated abruptness that Appleby fired off this question, and Punter detectably hesitated before replying. And when he did so, it was again by having recourse to his role.

'I hardly think it is my place, Sir John…'

'For heaven's sake, Mr Punter! Stop talking nonsense, and say what you have to say.'

'Thank you, sir. I know nothing of Mr Robin Carson. He appears to have been resident in America for some years, and I have gathered little as to either his disposition or his habits. It would hardly be my…'

'Quite so. Go on.'

'But I judge there is some reasonable cause for concern. Mrs Carson received, I understand, some specific information of his having arrived in this country – since when there has been silence.

And her apprehensions have been sharpened, it seems, by something she happened on in a newspaper.'

'What newspaper?'

'I have no idea, Sir John.' Punter produced this lie smoothly enough. 'I understand the account was of some wayside assault, or the like. Mrs Carson had reacted to it in a somewhat morbid fashion, supposing that her son was involved, and that he has very possibly been murdered. A most distressing aberration, Sir John.'

'No doubt. And Mr Carson?'

'He is also in some distress – and naturally so. But his own brief absence from Garford seems to me insignificant, and I have taken the liberty of suggesting to Mrs Carson that she need be in no anxiety about it. Business gentlemen have their sudden occasions, have they not?'

Appleby assented to this harmless generalization, and the walk down the corridor was resumed. Punter then opened the door of a small sitting-room.

'Sir John Appleby,' he said.

Mrs Carson was sitting in a window embrasure, weeping quietly into a handkerchief. She looked up, however, while Appleby was still standing in the doorway.

'Robin!' Mrs Carson cried. And on a lower note she repeated, 'Robin, Robin!'

This was disconcerting. If the unfortunate woman was capable of mistaking for her errant son a retired policeman with a good deal of *gravitas* in his comportment she must indeed be in a bad way. But Appleby then saw that this was a misconception. Cynthia Carson was as yet scarcely aware of his presence. She had simply been calling out to empty air. It didn't greatly improve matters.

'Good afternoon,' Appleby said, advancing into the room. 'I do hope you won't consider my call intrusive. I happened to be with the Chief Constable when you rang up his office, and he explained the state of the case to me. Colonel Pride and I are old friends.'

'How very kind!' Mrs Carson was, after a fashion, pulling herself together. 'I have been sure from the first, Sir John, that you can help me. Having been the Commissionaire, you know. And the local policeman, too.'

'We will do all we can.' Appleby rather doubted whether Tommy Pride would much care for this description of himself. 'The Chief Constable is determined to take charge of the situation in person, and we may expect him to arrive here at any minute. And also Humphry Lely. I have an idea he may be able to help us.'

'Mr Lely – the painting gentleman?'

'Yes, the painting gentleman.' Mrs Carson, Appleby supposed, was, like her husband, from an unassuming background. Under stress it showed through. Appleby found himself, of a sudden, feeling extremely sorry for Mrs Carson – foolish though her talk could be about dear little spots near St Vincent. He had to remind himself that he felt sorry for her husband as well. The one anguished parent deserved as much sympathy as the other. In a very unofficial way, both of them were now in a sense his clients. It was up to him – or to himself and Tommy jointly – to deliver them the goods in the person of their abducted son. But Carson was on the job before them, and in a manner it would be a shade awkward for the police to know about officially. The whole affair was difficult.

And now Mrs Carson was weeping anew. She had returned, in fact, to what Punter termed a distraught condition. Appleby waited in silence. He couldn't, he had decided, put an arm round the woman's shoulders in a grandfatherly way. And presently she at least became articulate again.

'Robin!' she cried. 'Darling, darling Robin – what have they done to you? They've murdered you, they've murdered you! I *know* they have.' Mrs Carson wrung her hands. 'And Carl too, of course.'

Appleby felt himself stiffen from top to toe. Than these last five words he positively felt that he had never heard anything odder in his life. Of course Mrs Carson was insane, and one must expect to be surprised by her. But what he had heard uttered with a complete naivety was simply an afterthought which the speaker judged that propriety required. And that telephone call to the police which Tommy had been apprised of while talking to Appleby was now instantly manifest as falling within the same category. It wasn't exactly that Cynthia didn't care two hoots for her Carl or what had happened to him. It was rather that her anxieties there were floating and uncertain; were active, it might be said, only at a superficial level of her mind. Her single deep and constant passion was that long-absent son who had failed to turn up on her. Appleby was still digesting this discovery when the door opened and Punter took a single step over its threshold.

'Colonel Pride and Mr Lely!' Punter shouted. The effect was of a man participating in a moment of high drama. But what was actually in question was merely the routine beloved by all stage butlers and many real ones.

And Tommy and the painting gentleman entered the room.

These further callers had presumably arrived simultaneously, and were being admitted by Punter because Appleby had mentioned they were turning up. So poor Mrs Carson was now 'receiving' in quite a big way. Commendably aware of social duty, she rang a bell and suggested to Mrs Punter that it might be nice to have a cup of tea. Appleby, who remembered the butler's wife only vaguely, took a searching look at her and – as it might be expressed – wrote her out of the story; something he was far from doing with Punter himself.

Humphry Lely, who had no idea why Appleby had telephoned asking him to turn up at Garford, was amiably silent. It was otherwise with the Chief Constable, who took charge at once. He might have been reflecting that although he would be unsurprised to find Appleby seeing a little further into this odd affair than he did, he himself had official responsibilities which, having taken them upon himself, he mustn't shirk. Tommy (Appleby thought) was rather like a consultant physician who, having been called in to a distressed household, mustn't forget to begin with routine reassurance before getting down to the job.

'My dear madam,' Tommy said briskly, 'I do greatly sympathize with you in your present anxieties. But I am confident – and am sure that Sir John agrees with me in this – that the situation can be controlled. Candour is what is essential. That achieved, we can see to it that neither your husband or your son comes to any serious harm.'

'They've murdered my Robin. I'm sure of it.' Mrs Carson had produced her handkerchief again, and appeared to remember something. 'And now Carl as well.'

'I beg you to compose yourself. It is our opinion – for I must be entirely frank with you – that something very shocking and deeply criminal has occurred. But the very character of what is being attempted makes your son's safety virtually certain for the present. Nor, I believe, is your husband at any grave risk. And his safety will be similarly assured as soon as we are able to contact him and gain his co-operation.'

This was a somewhat formal speech, and remote from Tommy Pride's more familiar manner of address. He probably employed it when dealing with Watch Committees and their like. Appleby felt that poor Mrs Carson might be bewildered and intimidated by it. But in fact she had an ear for what could be called the sound of a thing, and she responded favourably to Pride's note of authority. It even made her acute.

'So they haven't killed my Robin?' she asked. 'He has just been kidnapped for money for something like that?'

'As we see the matter, Mrs Carson, it is almost certainly so.'

'Then what about...what about the other one?' For a moment Mrs Carson's intermittent vagueness appeared to have overtaken her: it was almost as if she had forgotten her husband's name. 'What about my dear Carl?'

'It is really a little soon to say. Mr Carson, after all, has not been absent from Garford for very long. But it seems likely that he is endeavouring to secure his son's freedom by what he conceives to be the quickest method available to him.'

'And on that, it is very probable that Mr Lely can help us.' Appleby had interrupted with this, and he now turned to the painter. 'Humphry, can you lead us to that drawer?'

'That drawer?' It was only for a moment that Lely was at a loss. 'The one, you mean, with all those bank notes in it? Why, yes. It's in a great big bogus Jacobean affair in the library.' Lely had the grace to look uncomfortable at having produced this derogatory description of what was perhaps a cherished Carson heirloom. 'I never saw so much instant cash in my life, and I was far from quarrelling with it. I can take you to it straight away.'

'Then – with your permission, Mrs Carson – we'll all move to the library.' As he said this, Appleby strode to the door and opened it – sufficiently rapidly to afford a glimpse of Punter withdrawing hastily round a corner. 'Your butler,' he said dryly, 'shows a very active concern in your family affairs. Let's go.'

So they all moved to the library. It was a large and oppressive apartment which turned more congenially into a billiard room at its far end.

'Just like Castle Drogo,' Lely said cheerfully and admiringly. This was apparently by way of making amends for his previous remark. But he promptly added, 'One of poor old Lutyens' more absurd wheezes, that.'

Mrs Carson plainly didn't make much of this. Whether there is something unholy in contriving wedlock between a library and a billiard room was a problem that would not have occurred to her. But she at once pointed to what they were looking for.

'Would that be it?' she asked. 'I don't know what Carl keeps in it. The big drawer is always locked, so perhaps it's money. But then why should he cash cheques with Mrs Rumble?'

'Mrs Rumble?' Appleby repeated.

'At the Post Office Stores. Mrs Rumble is a most obliging woman.'

'I see.' Appleby reflected that this imbecile degree of financial ignorance must be an irritating thing to have around the house. It almost inclined him to what he thought of as the Pride Hypothesis: Carson had simply enlisted his son's help and bolted from the woman. But it was a moment at which whimsy was out of place. He walked over to the imposing piece of furniture indicated. 'The bottom drawer's the biggest,' he said to Lely. 'Was it that one?'

'Yes – and absolutely stuffed.'

'Locked?'

'Yes. He produced a key, paid me out my whack, and then locked up again.'

'We'll see if it's locked now. Handles a little tricky for a fingerprint wallah, wouldn't you say, Tommy?'

The Chief Constable agreed. The entire cupboard was in blackened oak, elaborately carved. On its two drawers the handles consisted of scowling lions' heads in deep relief, and one had to stick one's fingers within their maws to pull the drawers open. Appleby performed this operation on the deeper drawer at once. It opened easily. And it was quite empty.

'As one expected.' Appleby turned to Mrs Carson. 'May I explain this matter as I see it? Your husband had collected a very large sum of money in this drawer: almost certainly, many thousands of pounds. And bonds and the like too, perhaps, as well as currency. He may even have had similar caches elsewhere. Indeed, it's very likely; it would be the prudent thing to do. And yesterday he packed all this into suitcases and left Garford without telling you what he was about. Very thoughtfully, that is, he refrained from alarming you.'

'About Robin having been, you say, kidnapped?' Surprisingly, Mrs Carson appeared to have arrived dead on the ball. 'But ought Carl not to have gone straight to the police? Colonel Pride, isn't that right? Wouldn't you have got Robin back to us?'

Although this was a tricky question, with delicate issues involved, the Chief Constable hesitated only for a moment.

'It would, I think, have been best. I've already said as much, you know. It's most desirable that we should act in concert.'

'And not just pay up?'

'Precisely so. At the same time, I do sympathize with your husband's difficulty. He has no doubt received threats from the kidnappers that going to the police might not be – well, in the interest of his son's safety.'

'It's the obvious threat for kidnappers to employ.' Appleby took up this dire and awkward point forthrightly. 'It's almost common form with them, one may say. But we mustn't take too dark a view of it. It usually, I can assure you, remains an idle threat merely. Kidnappers, unless they are very amateur and bungling ones, don't in practice proceed to homicide.'

There was a short silence here, with Mrs Carson no doubt extracting what dubious comfort she could from these assurances. It was broken by Humphry Lely.

'What a ghastly mess!' Lely exclaimed impulsively. 'I'd no idea what we were involved with. Isn't this chap – isn't Mr Carson, I ought to say – in a pretty vulnerable position – wandering the countryside trying to hand over bags of money to a lot of crooks?' The question was more cogent than tactful so far as the unfortunate Mrs Carson was concerned. Lely seemed suddenly to realize this. 'At least I call it bloody courageous of him,' he added.

'It certainly is that.' Appleby, although he couldn't quite have said why, offered this agreement a shade thoughtfully. And he turned to Pride. 'I don't think I told you,' he said, 'that I had a call from a young man called Pluckworthy. He seems to work for Carson in some sort of secretarial capacity. Would that be right?' Appleby had turned to Carson's wife.

'Yes, indeed, Sir John. Dear Peter! He is quite devoted to Carl. I think he helps him a great deal with his affairs. He is very much a *confidential* secretary. And he has been extremely kind. Telling me not to be alarmed.'

'It seems to be his line – or one of his lines.' Appleby had turned to Pride again. 'As I've told you, I couldn't quite make him out. He ran the boys-will-be-boys notion: Robin will turn up on his parents when other attractions are exhausted – something like that. But there was an undercurrent to his talk. If the police – meaning you and me – barged in, there might be the hell of a mess. It was almost as if he were plugging at me the kidnapping situation we're now pretty clear about.'

'And anxious we'd keep away from it?' Pride asked. 'I don't know that I like the sound of him.'

At this moment the library door opened, and Punter again presented himself But, this time, he spoke wholly without enthusiasm.

'Mr Pluckworthy,' Punter mumbled grumpily.

And Peter Pluckworthy entered the room.

It wasn't clear whether Carl Carson's factotum had been made aware that Cynthia Carson was entertaining visitors. Certainly he showed no sign of discomposure. He walked straight up to the lady and kissed her affectionately – a salute that she appeared to receive in good part. This achieved, he turned to Appleby with a familiar and cheerful nod, and then to Pride – clearly the senior of the two remaining men – as if waiting to be introduced. This ceremony, however, not coming into Mrs Carson's head, was performed by Appleby.

'Colonel Pride, our Chief Constable.'

'How do you do, sir?' It appeared that Pluckworthy was minding his manners, and he took no injudicious initiative in offering to shake hands. Then he turned towards Lely, whom he may only have glimpsed so far, and instantly – if only briefly – his self-possession appeared to desert him.

'I rather think…' he began.

'Yes, of course. It's certainly me. Ages since we met.' Lely's cordiality seemed to Appleby a shade emphatic, and the consequence of a resolution quickly formed. 'In the great world of business, Pluckworthy? Lucky chap.'

'Lely and I were at school together.' Pluckworthy now offered this information easily and to the company at large, and then turned back to Mrs Carson. 'Cynthia, darling, I've dropped in only for a moment. Just to see how you are, and find out if you have any news.'

'Peter, it's too dreadful!' Mrs Carson was feeling for her handkerchief again. 'These gentlemen think that Robin has been captured by bandits, and I think they may have killed him. And now Carl has gone away with a great deal of money without telling anybody, and taking my car too. We none of us know what to think.'

This last assertion failed to please Pride.

'At least we are trying,' the Chief Constable said. 'And perhaps, Mr Pluckworthy, you can help us. I gather that you have already discussed the situation with Sir John Appleby. But Sir John was left without any clear sense of what was in your mind.'

'I'm sorry about that, sir. Perhaps I did rather change ground. I wanted to put the point that it might all be something of a false alarm. But then there was the possibility of a kidnapping. I wanted to emphasize that the police have to be very cautious in the face of that.'

'It was most kind of you, Mr Pluckworthy.' The Chief Constable could not have been more frigid.

'But now, I just don't know.'

Colonel Pride was plainly not interested in what Mr Pluckworthy didn't know. But Appleby was.

'Could you possibly,' Appleby asked, 'expand on that?'

'Well, I don't know that I can.' Pluckworthy appeared distressed. 'I'm in a bit of a muddle, really. But all that money! I can tell you – in confidence, of course – that the amount of cash Carl has been raising is really rather staggering. All that about the kidnapping: it seems pretty circumstantial, if you ask me. But I just wonder... I say, Cynthia, I must be off. I must, really.' And with this obscure speech, Peter Pluckworthy bolted from the room.

The conference broke up, and for a few minutes Appleby and Humphry Lely stood beneath the portico of Garford House together.

'Altogether rather rum,' Appleby said. 'That chap seems to specialize in disorderly retreats. And I have a notion, Humphry, that you know rather more about him than I do.'

'We were at school together – as he told us. I was two or three years his senior.'

'Well?'

'I don't know that you need "Well" at me. That's all that's to it.'

'It's nothing of the kind. Humphry. You had to decide to make friendly noises to him.'

'Well, yes. One mustn't humiliate a chap, if one can help it. The school turfed him out.'

'Expelled him?'

'Just that. It was an archaic sort of school. They might well have birched him first.'

'Had he seduced the matron?'

'Lord, no! That wouldn't have worried anybody. He was a bit too interested in other boys' wallets and pockets in the changing-rooms. Squalid and petty, wouldn't you say?'

'Definitely. But he may have been trading up since.' Appleby paused on this. 'By the way, Humphry, I've had it in mind to ask you a question. It's about the occasion of Carson's last sitting for his portrait. He told you something about Robin's coming home. Just what was it?'

'He'd had a cable about it, but hadn't yet told his wife.'

'That was it. Thank you very much.'

'I don't think he said anything more. So it wasn't a very communicative remark.'

'I suppose not. But one never knows.' Appleby looked thoughtfully at his companion. 'Tommy Pride,' he said inconsequently, 'likes to talk about leaving no stone unturned.'

'It must be easy enough when it's just a question of a boulder or two. But what about a beach full of pebbles?' Lely seemed rather pleased with this. 'I'd have no notion where to start, myself. All seems bewilderment. But do keep me informed.'

'I'm next to all bewilderment myself, Humphry. Through utter and through middle darkness borne: that's me.'

'Is that a way of saying there begins to be a glimmer – a chink of light, as they say, at the end of the tunnel?'

'After a fashion, yes, Humphry. But I have an awkward feeling that what the glimmer may reveal is the existence in my ageing head of some radical misconception. It's an almost purely intuitive feeling, and therefore thoroughly unsatisfactory. Shall I tell you what is my nastiest recurrent dream?'

'Heaven forbid!'

'But I shall. It's of playing a game that's all snakes and no ladders.'

15

'Is that you, John?' It was Pride's voice coming sharply over the line.

'Yes, it's me.'

'Have Judith and you had your dinner?'

'Yes. Roast chicken and some of those small sausages. Claret.'

'Good! I've waited until you'd had a chance to fortify yourself. Before, you know, reporting a disturbing development.'

'Not about the Carsons?'

'Yes, indeed: your wretched Carsons.'

'They're as much your Carsons as they're mine, Tommy.'

'Fair enough. Well, now. I thought I'd look in here – at my confounded office, that is – on my way home from our jolly Garford party. And they had this thing waiting for me. Shall I recount it?'

'Yes, of course. It's why you've rung me up.'

'I feel like the messenger chappie in those old plays. *The Fall of the House of Aeschylus*, and so forth. Know what I mean?'

'Just.'

'All violence takes place off stage, and one character passes it on to another in a cosy chat. This is our second. And it's *da capo*, more or less.'

'Not another kidnap?'

'Just that – if it isn't merely robbery with violence and a spot of murder thrown in. And the astonishing thing is they know about the blood already. Those back-room wallahs once more.'

'Tommy, the messenger usually begins at the beginning. For instance, he may briefly sketch, or at least indicate, the location. Would it be near Heathrow again?'

'Not. Very much not near anywhere at all. A blasted heath.'

'In Scotland?'

'The Berkshire moors – where the dons met the gipsy. Fly our greetings, fly our speech and smiles. An ideally secluded spot, they tell me, for a quiet hand over of assets. I'm being taken for a look-see at first light. Care to come?'

'I think not.'

'Oh.'

'Remember Mycroft Holmes, Tommy? He's Sherlock's lethargic brother. He sits at home and thinks things out, while young Sherlock scurries round in hansom cabs, or crawls about on carpets, brandishing a magnifying glass. In old age I'm going to be Mycroft. I've only just thought of it. But the decision is irrevocable.'

'Calming me down, aren't you, John?'

'Well, yes. But go on telling me. How detailedly was it a repeat? Was there a little man in a Mini?'

'Absolutely not. No spectatorship. Just signs of a stiff struggle, it seems. Including the blood. But it all mightn't have been noticed for days if Mrs Carson's car hadn't been spotted overturned in a ditch a couple of hundred yards away.'

'And two empty suitcases?'

'Just that.'

'Now tell me what they say about the blood.'

'It's absolutely amazing. Even after the stuff's clotted, and so on, it appears they can do all their tests on it. So it was rushed to the appropriate boffin, and within ten minutes he knew there was something special about it. It belongs to an exceedingly rare blood group, or whatever the term is. Then they got on to Carson's leech, who chose to see the thing as an emergency, and named Carson's blood group at once. And the two match. That's pretty conclusive, is it not?'

'Yes… Yes, I rather think it is.'

Appleby's voice had changed oddly, and for some seconds there was silence on the line.

'John?'

'Sorry, Tommy. Just poor old Mycroft thinking like mad. Will you try to discover something for him?'

'Of course.'

'I haven't a notion whether it's easy, or plain impossible. But I want to know whether, in the week or thereabout before Lely finished Carson's portrait, Carson received a cable from America.'

16

For over a week nothing whatever happened that might throw light on the fate of Carl Carson. For two or three days his disappearance in sinister circumstances was a sensation, rating a middling-prominent spread in the popular newspapers. The police were reported as finding themselves 'baffled'. And this didn't mean, as it sometimes does, that the police knew all about the affair and were just waiting to pounce. It was literally true. The papers also announced that the police saw no reason to connect 'the Berkshire mystery' (as it was being called) with an earlier episode of obscure wayside violence also in Berkshire, but near Heathrow. This was a lie, although not a particularly useful one: it was given out in the persuasion that a few lies *ought* to be given out when anything rather ticklish is in question. One paper, more enterprising than the others, darkly hinted that what was involved was an episode of ruthless 'gang warfare'. This was definitely taking a risk in the interest of a gratified readership, its underlying assumption being that Carson was dead. If he was alive and capable of turning up more or less blamelessly in one or another corner of the land, he would certainly be able to launch a libel action as having been aspersed as a gang-warfare type.

Colonel Pride communicated with Sir John Appleby every day. He appeared to feel that, if not on Tuesday, then at least on Wednesday, the solution of the whole thing would emerge fully formed from Appleby's head, much in the manner of whatever her name was from the head of Zeus. Appleby, on his part, from time to time suggested that Pride should attempt to find out this or that. Was Mrs Carson, for example, a woman with a substantial private fortune? It seemed unlikely. On one occasion she had offered Appleby some remark suggesting an almost imbecile ignorance of the difference between big money and petty cash. But one never knew. Perhaps quite long ago her husband had prudently managed to settle on her a large capital sum without her even having become clearly aware of the fact. Many men of his sort did something of the kind as a precaution against future drastic financial embarrassment.

Pride quite understood this point. The kidnappers, he saw, had double-crossed Carl Carson. They had been able to do so because the man had behaved pretty well in as dotty a way as might have been achieved by his loopy wife. What commonly happens in such kidnapping cases is that the fellow who has to pay up is instructed to put the cash in his car, drive to a named public telephone kiosk, and await an incoming call at a definite hour. He is then told to move on to another telephone: and this happens several times, thus enabling the kidnappers to check on whether he is being trailed by the police. Finally, he is told to drive to some unfrequented spot, conceal the money, drive away, and hope for the best. But this hadn't happened in the present case. The kidnappers had simply met the man, violently assaulted him, and made off with both him and his money-bags.

Why? Either, Pride told himself, because Carson had somehow found out too much about his adversaries to be let go free, or because they hoped to begin the ransom racket all over again. In this latter case, they would sooner or later make some approach to Carson's wife – but this they would do only if believing that there was still big money in the Carson kitty.

Pride did see that there were difficulties in accepting this. He inclined to the view that Carl Carson was dead – and that the man's unfortunate son was dead too. It wasn't a nice picture. He was really hoping that Appleby would somehow wave a wand over it and produce something at least marginally less disagreeable.

Appleby, it might be said, was doing his best. He paid a further call on Cynthia Carson, and tried to set her talking informatively on several subjects upon which he notably lacked information. Who were her husband's chief friends and associates? Had any new ones turned up recently? Had she happened to notice him as worried or preoccupied when letters or telephone calls had come to him? Did she remember any previous occasions upon which he had absented himself from home suddenly and without explanation? Had he lately placed any emphasis on the desirability of domestic economies?

None of this got Appleby very far. It couldn't have been said of Mrs Carson that she was taciturn or reticent; she talked quite a lot; but the conception that questions were framed in the hope of eliciting answers seemed to be quite outside her grasp. But Appleby persevered. Inconsequence can sometimes be as revealing as relevance. It was in the middle of speaking (rather perplexingly) about a dairy herd that Mrs Carson mentioned as among her present anxieties the fact that she would have 'nothing to fall back on'. And launched for the moment on this, she was further communicative. It had, she said, always been so. She had met Carl as a widow 'not well left', and he had been obliged to pay even for her wedding clothes. Carl, she explained with no particular enthusiasm, was a most generous man, and he had never required her 'to have any dealings with the money'.

So here was one question responded to beyond expectation – and to another, rather surprisingly, Appleby got a direct answer. Mrs Carson explained that, because Carl liked to have everything around him obviously in a prosperous condition, he had been a little inclined to suggest that his wife was something of an heiress.

'It was a very generous attitude,' Appleby said with aplomb. His past life, he reflected, was littered with just such ghastly professional prevarications. 'But would it have become a general view of your circumstances? Let me see. Take a man like your butler. I forget his name.'

'Punter.'

'Of course – Punter. Would Punter be inclined to think of you as a wealthy woman?'

'Oh, yes – I think so. Mrs Punter has said things rather suggesting that. But I don't want to talk about Punter. He has been rather funny lately.'

'Funny?'

'Yes, nasty. Did I say funny? I meant nasty. As if he had something waiting for me.'

'Would it be as if he were proposing to get you under his thumb?'

'Oh, yes – just that.' Mrs Carson gave this assent with alarming and senseless gaiety. 'How interesting that you should know about Punter!'

'I think I'd like to know a little more. I'll drop in on him as I go out.'

Punter was sitting in his pantry, with a glass of what might have been Madeira in front of him. He had admitted Appleby to the house with his normal comportment, but now he didn't get to his feet. It was as if he had instantly sensed a changed relationship.

'I intend to ask you some questions,' Appleby said.

'The hell you do! Who do you think you are? Pretending to be a policeman again?'

This was interesting. Appleby decided that, so far as Garford House went, Punter was on the eve of asking for his cards. Presumably accompanied by his wife, he proposed to leave those proud towers to swift destruction doomed. But, first, he was going to treat himself to a little insolence all round. Appleby took no exception to this. It would make it the easier to get the man off-balance.

'No,' Appleby said. 'You may reassure yourself I don't intend to turn policeman again.'

'Then you've no business here. Clear out, Mr Nosy Parker.'

'If I clear out, the police move in. They'll be interested in putting you in gaol, my friend. I am not. So you're in luck that it is I who am in this room with you. I'm prepared to treat you as quite unimportant. And that's generous, wouldn't you say? But I do intend to have a little information from you.'

Punter considered these propositions in silence for some seconds. They were having an effect on his complexion. And when he sought to recruit himself from the glass in front of him, his hand wasn't quite steady. Appleby noted these signs with satisfaction.

'So here goes, Punter. Just why did you contrive to bring that newspaper paragraph to Mrs Carson's attention?'

'I don't know what you're talking about.' Punter was clearly a startled man.

'Come, come. We mustn't waste time. You were under observation, Punter.' Appleby said this as if an entire crime squad had been lurking round that arbour. 'But, if you like, I'll start elsewhere. You've only just discovered, haven't you, that Mrs Carson isn't worth a penny?'

'No more she is, the old bag. Nor Carson either, by now, if you ask me.'

'That is a most satisfactory reply. I'm pleased with you, Punter. And, now, an important question. You've been operating merely on the side, I take it? Yes or no.'

'Yes.' Punter's reply, if sulky, had been immediate.

Appleby had employed a technical expression, and the man had automatically responded to it.

'In some eavesdropping way, you got hold of the notion that Mr Robin Carson has been kidnapped. You decided to panic Mrs Carson into paying out money that would free him – without consulting her husband, and in some fashion that would land it quickly in your own pocket. It's a regular underworld trick, and it comes off surprisingly often. Speed and shock-tactics are, of course, the essence of it.'

'You seem to know a bloody lot.'

'Yes, I do. And what you didn't know is that Mrs Carson on her own doesn't command a bean. Right?'

Punter considered this with an incongruous effect of leisure.

'Yes' he said.

'In other words, you are an incompetent small-time crook. And that's the whole story. You actually know nothing whatever about what has happened either to Mr Robin Carson or to his father. Right?'

'Yes – Sir John.'

'What you will now do is this: you will go to Mrs Carson and, with proper respect, say that you and your wife are obliged to leave her service at once. Without, needless to say, any further payment of wages. You will then pack up and quit – both of you. Incidentally, I am acting very improperly in making this arrangement. It is simply that I am disinclined to have Mrs Carson suffer the disturbing spectacle of policemen huddling her butler in handcuffs into a van. Good morning.'

'So that's Punter,' Appleby said to Judith at lunchtime. 'An irrelevance, essentially, and not a very agreeable one at that.'

'And you're just allowing him to fade away?'

'Just that.'

'Isn't it rather letting him loose on society at large?'

'I suppose it might be viewed as that. But I haven't become an accessory after the fact, you know. There *isn't* any fact. One couldn't hope to make any charge stick on the man. It isn't a crime to ensure that a daft woman sees something in a newspaper.'

'So, in fact, your bullying him into confessing his design and agreeing to quit was just a bluff?'

'Absolutely so.'

'You're to be congratulated, John. And now you can get on with it. After the irrelevant, the relevant.'

'Yes, indeed. I wonder whether I might go over to Upton Grange and have a word with Mary Watling? I've rather hesitated about that. The Lelys brought the girl to tea, but we don't really know the Watlings very well. And I have no real standing in the affair. Colonel Watling is rather a high-metalled old chap, and might consider it a damned impertinence. Perhaps it had better be one of Pride's more tactful people.'

'I doubt whether the Watlings would much care to have a superior bobby inquiring into their daughter's behaviour. There seems to be a mystery about that, which the elder Watlings may be aware of and not greatly care for.'

'Precisely my own condition. Robin's mother told you that her son is engaged to the girl – whether formally or informally, we don't know – and that the engagement was his main reason for coming to England. That was the way of it, wasn't it?'

'I think it was, more or less. But it was only a telephone call, you'll remember. And the woman does talk in a wandering sort of fashion.'

'She does, indeed. And Mary Watling doesn't seem to talk at all. She said nothing whatever about it when the Lelys brought her here. She seemed not very much to like even a bare reference to Mrs Carson with her milk and superior potatoes, and the moment Robin himself was mentioned, she got up and wandered off into the garden.'

'I noticed that. It all suggests, John, that she mightn't greatly relish your politely inquisitive call.'

'I don't think I'd be worried by that. Here are grave matters more or less dumped on my lap, and here is young Miss Watling just possibly able to throw some light on them. Incidentally, if there's any truth whatever in the story of an engagement, or even attachment, she must have heard enough by now to be a very worried child. She might welcome me.'

'That's true. And you'd be two worried people together.'

Appleby appeared a little startled by this remark. He even got to his feet, walked to the window, and surveyed the garden. Solo was just visible, sitting on a barrow and waving his arms in the air. Did the boy want to be rescued from something? Was he, as in the poem, not waving but drowning? Appleby saw that Solo was merely at war with a wasp, bee, or harmless fly. He turned back to Judith.

'Yes,' he said, 'I'm more worried than I was. It comes of having a thought or two about what Tommy calls the second kidnap. There's something wrong about it. On the strength of our slight acquaintance with him, would you be inclined to call Carl Carson a guileless character?'

'Far from it.'

'Exactly so. Yet here he is, behaving with a kind of imbecile innocence that would do credit to his wife. He piles into a car a small fortune in a highly negotiable form, and drives off with it to keep a lonely rendezvous with some crooks. I ask you.' Appleby paused on this, rather as if surprised at having produced an uncharacteristic colloquialism. 'And the blood, Judith. The bloody blood!'

'Blood is bloody, I suppose – except on the stage, when it's a little bag of suitably tinted vinegar, waiting to be pricked by the villain's dagger.'

'It's that, is it? I've sometimes wondered. But the point about this blood is that it's pretty well unique. Could anything be more pat?'

'Be what?'

'P-a-t: *pat*. It's the sort of thing that just doesn't happen. Or not in real life. You might find it in a *roman policier*. Like that haemophiliac's blood somewhere in Dorothy Sayers.'

For a moment this reduced Lady Appleby to silence. It was the first intimation she had ever received of her husband's having read a detective story. And before she could speak, there was the sound of a telephone bell.

'That damned instrument's beginning to plague us,' Appleby said irritably. 'I'll take it.'

'John?'

'Yes, Tommy.'

'That cable. They've just traced it. Or, rather they haven't.'

'Explain.'

'It's amazing – isn't it – what the boffins can produce for one nowadays? Find a thing for you in no time. Find a non-thing in a matter of days. During the period you specified, Carl Carson received no cable, and no telephone call either, from America. What do you make of that?'

It was only for a second that Appleby had to search for an answer. 'A lot,' he said.

'What's that?'

'I think I make quite a lot of it. Any further development?'

'Not a thing. They've had a hundred men crawling over that patch of…'

'Of course they have. But not including Mycroft.'

'What's that?'

'No matter, Tommy. I'll be in contact with you again soon. And thank you very much.'

17

William Lockett was now installed as Hoobin's second assistant, and he turned up at Long Dream every day. That he bore at least a secondary character as what might be called a secret agent was a fact which had rapidly become barely dissimulated between his new employer and himself.

'Chaotic,' William reported to Appleby a couple of days after the disturbing discovery about the non-existent cable. 'That's us at bleeding Garford House. My dad's given his notice to the old girl, and he'll begin to draw his pension next week. We'll be out of the cottage, I reckon, as soon as that Pluckworthy gets his paws on the works and his snout in the trough.'

'Pluckworthy? Has Mrs Carson sent for him?'

'Yesterday, she did. She told my dad so. The ruddy Punters have cleared out like the place had been hit by the Black Death, and Mrs C doesn't know how to boil herself an egg. Forgotten about it, I suppose, since she joined the gentry. Born in a back-kitchen, is my dad's notion of Mrs C. And the late C himself, like enough.'

'Do you mean you think Mr Carson is dead?'

'It's the general notion, that. Pluckworthy's arriving today. The sorrowing widow says he'll pull things together. More likely he'll pocket the ancestral Carson silver, if you ask me. I've had about six words with him in my life, and I didn't like any of them. One of nature's wide boys is Pluckworthy.'

'There must be lawyers, William, who have some duty to protect Mrs Carson's interests.'

'They'll have a hard row to hoe, my dad would say. The woman's that moon-struck a man might be sorry for her.'

'Yes, I think a man might be that. If there's trouble about the cottage, William, let me know. There may be more law to that than they reckon on.'

'Sir,' William Lockett said, and went off to join Solo.

Peter Pluckworthy had been a good deal on Appleby's mind, and he had been inclined to think it highly desirable to contact him. Now it appeared possible to do so before the day was out. So, after tea, Appleby got in the car and drove over to Garford. It was Pluckworthy himself who answered the bell.

'Oh, hallo, Sir John,' he said. 'Do come in.' And he drew the door fully open with what was perhaps designed as a symbolic unreserve. 'Cynthia's lying down. She's in a sad way, poor soul. I've come over to help her if I can.'

'Perhaps you can help me too.'

'I'll be delighted.' Pluckworthy said this with a quick cordiality in which he himself appeared to be conscious of a false note. And he switched at once to something faintly sardonic. 'Am I to understand, Sir John, that you are what's called helping the police with their inquiries?'

'After a fashion, yes. They may be asking you to do it, too.'

'Then do come in.' Pluckworthy's eyes had narrowed. 'Let me get you a drink, and we'll have a chat.'

They went into the same small room in which Appleby had previously conferred on the perplexities of the Carson affair, and Pluckworthy at once fetched drinks. Appleby accepted this hospitality without demur, since to have declined might have seemed like a declaration of war which could yet prove wholly misconceived.

'Any police developments,' Pluckworthy asked easily, 'in this wretched affair?'

'I can tell you of one development at once. Your employer told a blank lie about Robin's heralding his arrival in England. He told

Humphry Lely, the man who painted his portrait, that he'd had a cable from his son. He hadn't.'

'And that's important?'

'To my mind, Mr Pluckworthy, it's like the rotating of a kaleidoscope. The whole picture changes. I have concluded that the entire story of kidnap and ransom is moonshine.'

If Sir John Appleby was astonished to hear himself say this (and he was), he had the satisfaction of seeing that Peter Pluckworthy was at least equally startled. Nevertheless, the young man's response was notably prompt.

'I'm afraid,' he said, 'that I have, too.'

'Then we can consider the matter together. Aren't you, by the way, rather prone to shifting ground?'

'I suppose one must follow the evidence as it discloses itself.' Pluckworthy delivered this composed and unexceptionable response on a note of mild surprise. 'About those kidnaps, you know: first one and then the other. I started off by judging the first of them perfectly genuine. Didn't you?'

'Yes.' Appleby realized that if here was an adversary, he was a formidable one. 'Go on.'

'I knew, for a start, that Carl had suddenly started desperately searching round for money. No, that's not quite right. Organizing the stuff. Of course, there was plenty of it there. But I saw that he wanted to get it on tap without attracting too much notice. There were reasons of simple commercial prudence for that.'

'No doubt.'

'But there was something more. There was something he didn't want to bring into public notice. I was working fairly closely with Carl, you know, and that was a fact I became thoroughly conscious of. Then when the business of Robin Carson's having failed to turn up became known to me, I felt the truth of the matter must be determined. So I tackled Carl about it. We had quite a tussle. But in the end I got the whole story. It was a pretty astonishing one. And what became chiefly clear to me was that, if it all came out, it was going to be uncommonly hard on Cynthia. I'm very fond of Cynthia.

Cynthia's been like a mother to me.' Pluckworthy paused on this, as if wondering whether it sounded quite right. 'Everything I've done or said since – and I'm afraid it has involved me in a certain amount of deception – has really been to protect her.'

Appleby received this in silence. He had been prompted to say something like, 'That's most edifying'. But he decided to keep mum.

'About that cable,' Pluckworthy said – apparently going off at a tangent. 'You've discovered there was no cable. It's unsurprising. You see, there's no Robin Carson, either.'

This time, Appleby had no need to counsel himself to silence. He was literally dumbfounded.

'Cynthia never had a son by Carl. Robin is a figment of her poor, disordered brain. And Carl – who's something of a saint in his way – has always simply gone along with it. Isn't that amazing?' Pluckworthy scarcely paused on this question. 'But there's more amazement to come.'

'I can certainly see a jury,' Appleby said, 'being astonished at such a yarn.'

'I rather think there won't be a jury. It seems to me – viewing the thing as a whole – that there won't be anybody to put before one.'

'I'll have to be convinced of that. Continue.'

'Carl's plan, of course, wasn't to ransom a non-existent young man. It was simply to get out of the country with as much cash as he could collect in a hurry. His affairs, you see, are in the hell of a mess.'

'More than just Mr Carson's affairs may be in a mess, if you ask me.'

'But this later development – kidnapping himself as well, you may call it – is really pretty ingenious, wouldn't you say? One sees the idea: an affair that went badly wrong, as kidnappings sometimes do. A regular balls-up: muddle, panic, murder and what have you. The villains, the fuzz will say, cut and run – but pleased enough since it was with the cash. We'll have to mount a hunt, they'll say, for a couple of bodies: father and son. But we shan't find them. They're down much too deep a well.'

'And where, according to this account of things, is Carl Carson now, Mr Pluckworthy?'

'Well on his way to Bolivia, or some such place. And with a pretty packet in his pocket.'

'His pocket? It can't be quite that.'

'True enough. Carl will have made some previous arrangements there. In a modest way, you know, he exports this and that all over the world. It's an area of British enterprise in which all sorts of funny business goes on. No problem.'

Appleby for some moments considered this extraordinary farrago or fandango in silence. Its strength, he saw, inhered in the fact that a good deal of it was probably true. But what it omitted was what he had to go for.

'Mr Pluckworthy, you charged yourself a few minutes ago with what you called, I think, a certain amount of deception. Aren't you doing yourself an injustice? You seem yourself to have provided nothing to the entertainment apart from a certain amount of generous feeling. Carson's behaviour, as you describe it, was undoubtedly criminal. There need be no mistake about that. And there are points at which he undoubtedly had an accomplice or accomplices. It is now known to the police that somebody flew from New York to London under the name of Robin Carson. It is known that somebody made a telephone call to Mrs Carson from Heathrow. The first kidnapping may have been a charade, and I think that on scrutiny it distinctly lacks verisimilitude. But it was a charade with two actors. I wonder whether your recollection would be at fault if you were to swear that you were not one of them?'

'And Carl himself the other one?'

'I didn't say so – and you make the point rather promptly.'

'If I helped Carl…'

'But you wouldn't have helped him if your devotion, as you maintain, was to his unfortunate wife. She is now left destitute, is she not?'

'If I helped Carl, you have to prove it.'

Pluckworthy had snapped this out to an effect of naked challenge which was perhaps a slip up on his part. He wasn't looking too happy. Just find another chink in this fellow's assurance, Appleby thought, and he's as good as a gonner.

'About that second affair, Mr Pluckworthy, in which Carson was to be supposed to have been double-crossed in some way, and then killed, I take it, in some not altogether plausible panic. We know, of course, that his wife's car was found close to the scene of a crime, together with two empty suitcases which were undoubtedly Carson's property. But we can't be assured, can we, that that second charade wasn't mounted with Carson himself, so to speak, *in absentia*, and Peter Pluckworthy rigging up the whole thing?'

'Of course we can! 'The blood...' Pluckworthy checked himself, but a fraction of a second too late.

'Yes, Mr Pluckworthy...the blood?'

'I don't know what you're talking about.'

'That, Mr Pluckworthy, is your first wholly futile remark. You are rather cracking up, you know – as you are likely to do in a witness box one day. You were about to tell me that the blood found on the spot was Carson's almost to a certainty. But that fact is most assuredly not common knowledge as yet. It can have come to you only from Carson himself: and a singularly foolish projected ingenuity it was. It's of no vast importance, perhaps. But it does serve to show how closely involved you must have been with the whole bizarre and unquestionably criminal project from its inception. And now, I think you may expect matters to develop fairly rapidly. My friend Colonel Pride, who is Chief Constable of what I believe is now called the region, is dealing with the matter himself And he has a brisk military way with him.'

'You can go to hell.'

'That is less futile than merely bankrupt, is it not? Bankruptcy, incidentally, is what the disreputable Carl Carson, it seems, was on the verge of when he thought up all this nonsense. Where I shall now go, actually, is to the police. Later, I may return here, and have a difficult encounter with an unfortunate lady. In the interval, you will have to decide whether to make a bolt for it, or to stay put and try to brazen things out. A hard decision for you, is it not? Good evening to you.'

18

'Extraordinary!' Tommy Pride said. 'Never heard anything like it.'

'It certainly presents some unusual features.'

'Dashed ingenious, I must say.'

'Too ingenious to make much sense.'

'Would you say, John, it was Carson's plan – or essentially this fellow Pluckworthy's?'

'Carson's, I think. Just as Pluckworthy represents it to have been.'

'And Carson has got away with it?'

'Literally that. Carson's probably on the other side of the Atlantic by now. And the "it" includes a tidy little fortune following him by what's called long sea.'

'Most unfortunate. Caught with our pants down – eh? But I suppose we can nobble Pluckworthy.'

'Almost certainly. He may have gone off to lie low for a bit, and think out his way round his more awkward corners. But I doubt whether he'll decide to made a permanent fugitive of himself. It mayn't be altogether easy to hit on just what to charge him with. And even if you manage that, and get a conviction, it mayn't go very hard with him. And he has probably secured a modest rake off on the whole venture.'

The Chief Constable acquiesced in this with a nod, and devoted a few seconds to silent gloom.

'Do you know?' he said. 'What worries me most is the position of Carson's wretched wife. Of course, she must be as daft as a coot. Imagining she had a son! Quite an unheard-of thing.'

But here Appleby shook his head.

'I believe not. It does occur – mostly with childless women who are otherwise unhinged as well. I believe the Carsons had a family. Girls, I seem to have been told, who died or were killed in an accident. Something like that.'

'I suppose the poor lady's booked for the bin. Shocking thing, every way on. Mitigates Carson's rascality in some degree, wouldn't you say? The strain of it.'

Colonel Pride, a determinedly liberal-minded man, looked hopefully at Appleby.

'I can't say I see it just like that, Tommy.' Appleby got to his feet. 'Anyway, I'm going back to Garford now to see if I can be of any use to the woman.'

'And I'll get the hooks out for this bloody little Peter Pluckworthy Esquire. Know anything about his stable?'

'Not much. Public school. Like the mythical Robin, who was a Groton and Harvard boy.'

'Worse and worse, John!' And Tommy Pride made a gesture of despair. 'One just asks oneself: what are things coming to?'

Dusk had fallen by the time Appleby reached Garford House. Halfway up the drive, he braked abruptly and stared unbelievingly ahead of him. For a moment he thought the place was on fire. He even told himself with momentary conviction that Pluckworthy, as a valedictory gesture, had contrived arson on a large scale. Then he saw that it wasn't quite so dramatic as that. It was simply that the house was a blaze of light. The stuff was streaming from a dozen tall, uncurtained windows. Incongruously into his head there came a memory of how, in the early years of his marriage, Judith and he would drive up at night to a house like this in which a ball was getting under way. Mrs Carson was putting on a turn; was endeavouring, so to speak, to illuminate in this random fashion her own darkened state of mind. Appleby drove rapidly on to the house, drew up, jumped from his car, and ran up a flight of steps. He had scarcely rung the bell before the front door was flung upon and the brightly lit hall was

before him. He glimpsed the displeasing female statues in their
niches. But immediately in front of him, momentarily unidentifiable
because in mere silhouette, was a living woman, a breathless and
excited girl.

'Sir John!' the girl cried out. 'How absolutely splendid. Come in,
come in. We're calling it a party.'

It was Mary Watling, mysteriously transported to the Carson
home, and like Mrs Carson apparently out of her mind. But she was
merely radiant. Without waiting for a word, she led the way into the
nearest room, which was also the drawing-room and principal
apartment in the house. At the party there didn't appear to be many
guests. What Appleby first saw, indeed, wasn't people at all but on a
table a couple of bottles of champagne. Then he found that there was
a young man: a tall and handsome young man distinguishably of an
athletic rather than an intellectual sort. And there was Cynthia
Carson, who promptly flung herself into Appleby's arms.

'At last, at last!' she cried. 'He has come at last. Robin, my son.'

Much as if he and the champagne had been for some time
acquainted, Appleby felt his head swim. He stared at the young man.

'Robin Carson?' he said.

'Not exactly that, I guess.' The young man was smiling easily, was
even laughing in a good humoured way. 'Robin Hood, sir – and
happy to know you.'

'*Robin Hood?*'

And Mrs Carson explained. It was with an odd, momentary poise
and dignity.

'My first husband was called Hood,' she said. 'He was a realtor, Sir
John. He topped the tree over a wide region in making real estate
more thoroughly a commodity than it was in any other part of the
States.' It was on a nostalgic note that Mrs Carson revived these
memories of grandeur. 'My poor Carl knew very little of Mr Hood.'

'I just had to send a cable,' Mary Watling explained. 'It was all
becoming too difficult. I often simply didn't know what to say.
Because of Robin's being thought of, being so *generally* thought of' –

and here Mary glanced cautiously at the eccentric person who was presumably her future mother-in-law – 'as Mr Carson's son.'

'It was a kindness,' Mrs Carson said. Mrs Carson was now entirely calm. 'Robin, dear, will you give Sir John a glass of the champagne? It was a kindness to poor Carl, who did so want a son, always to speak as if he were Robin's father. I don't think Carl ever quite *understood* about Robin. He was rather *strange* about it all. I sometimes think – naturally, I am speaking *quite* confidentially – that Carl was just a tiny bit mad. But Carl is dead now, you know. Just like Mr Hood. Carl is definitely dead. So we can all be open and comfortable.'

'I just had to send a cable,' Mary Watling was repeating. 'And Robin managed to get away. He is terribly involved in his business affairs. But he managed to fly over at once. Isn't it wonderful?'

'It is certainly most remarkable.' Appleby's chief concern was not to look with open commiseration at this girl, so blithely proposing to bear Cynthia Carson's grandchildren. 'And I hope you will be very happy.' It occurred to him that he had better shake hands with Robin Hood again, and felicitate him as well. And this he managed to do. He wondered what on earth could have been the young man's history: the origin, growth and progress of the weird deception in which he had been involved. He'd never know. Nor, for that matter, did he much want to. He wondered whether he ought to say something to Cynthia Carson about the husband she had just, in effect, so comfortably buried. Far from being dead, Carl Carson was probably in South America by now, comfortably awaiting the arrival of his smuggled fortune. Appleby decided to say nothing. It would spoil the party.

'I'm only sorry dear Peter Pluckworthy isn't here,' Mrs Carson was saying. 'I don't know why, but he had to go away in a hurry.'

Sir John Appleby was a conscientious man, and it was midnight before he arrived home at Dream. As not at Garford, the house was in darkness. Judith would long before have gone to bed. He put the car away, entered the house quietly, and made his way upstairs. He was already in his pyjamas when he heard the telephone ring below.

Cursing inwardly, he went down and answered it.

'Detective-Inspector Davidson speaking,' a formal voice said. 'I have the Chief Constable's instructions, even although the hour be inconvenient, to speak to Sir John Appleby.'

'Speaking, Mr Davidson.'

'We found the body, sir, this afternoon.'

'The body! Whose body?' For a moment – for it was after a long day – a most improper irritation overcame Appleby. 'What the devil do you mean?'

'The body of the man Carl Carson, sir. I had a hundred men searching every inch…'

'Of course you had. Well?'

'I drafted in another hundred, and extended the radius of the search. It paid off.' For a moment there was a hint of satisfaction in the matter-of-fact voice on the line. 'They found the well.'

'The *well*?'

'Or rather the whole obsolete system, Sir John. Empty cisterns and exhausted wells. It appears that, many years ago, there was a large-scale attempt to divert the water through the chalk. That kind of thing.'

'Yes?'

'There are five wells in all. I had a man down every one of them. The body was at the bottom of the last and deepest of the lot. Carson had been shot through the back of the head. And then through the body – which accounts for the large effusion of blood.'

'It would.'

'Formal identification will take place tomorrow. But, of course, there is no doubt about it. None whatever.'

'There wouldn't be, no.' Appleby felt that this wasn't a particularly bright remark. Detective-Inspector Davidson was being extremely respectful. He knew the almost legendary person to whom he was talking. But he might very well be telling himself that the old boy was probably a bit past it. And perhaps he was right. Appleby felt that he ought to have kept better tabs on the gentleman referred to by Tommy Pride as Peter Pluckworthy Esquire. 'And have you anything further to report?' he asked – and was at once conscious that 'report' hadn't been quite right. He was being kept informed.

'Yes, Sir John. A telephone message from London only half an hour ago. They've got him.'

'Pluckworthy?'

'Yes. In his flat. He'd just got back there, and was packing up like mad. If it can be called packing. Just enormous sums of money. The picture's pretty clear, isn't it? He was this Carson's accomplice all the way through. Had been, indeed, what you might call his confidential agent for some years. Would he have been the master mind, would you say, in this entire swindle?'

'I'd say you have yet to find out.' Appleby was cautious. 'But he certainly came within an ace of bringing off a pretty piece of treachery in the end. He'd have managed it, Mr Davidson, but for your very efficient conduct of the operation. I congratulate you.'

'Thank you, Sir John.'

'I'll be seeing the Chief Constable fairly soon, no doubt. Please give him my compliments, meanwhile.'

'Certainly, Sir John.'

'And a message. Tell him that Mycroft has retired.'

'Sir?'

'That Mycroft has retired.'

'Very good, Sir John. Message understood.'

MICHAEL INNES

APPLEBY AT ALLINGTON

Sir John Appleby dines one evening at Allington Park, the Georgian home of his acquaintance, Owain Allington, who is new to the area. His curiosity is aroused when Allington mentions his nephew and heir to the estate, Martin Allington, whose name Appleby recognises. The evening comes to an end but, just as Appleby is leaving, they find a dead man – electrocuted in the *son et lumière* box that had been installed in the grounds.

APPLEBY ON ARARAT

Inspector Appleby is stranded on a very strange island, with a rather odd bunch of people – too many men, too few women (and one of them too attractive) cause a deal of trouble. But that is nothing compared to later developments, including the body afloat in the water and the attack by local inhabitants.

'Every sentence he writes has flavour, every incident flamboyance'
– *Times Literary Supplement*

MICHAEL INNES

THE DAFFODIL AFFAIR

Inspector Appleby's aunt is most distressed when her horse, Daffodil – a somewhat half-witted animal with exceptional numerical skills – goes missing from her stable in Harrogate. Meanwhile, Hudspith is hot on the trail of Lucy Rideout, an enigmatic young girl who has been whisked away to an unknown isle by a mysterious gentleman. And when a house in Bloomsbury, supposedly haunted, also goes missing, the baffled policemen search for a connection. As Appleby and Hudspith trace Daffodil and Lucy, the fragments begin to come together and an extravagant project is uncovered, leading them to a South American jungle.

'Yet another surprising firework display of wit and erudition and ingenious invention'
– *Guardian*

DEATH AT THE PRESIDENT'S LODGING

Inspector Appleby is called to St Anthony's College, where the President has been murdered in his Lodging. Scandal abounds when it becomes clear that the only people with any motive to murder him are the only people who had the opportunity – because the President's Lodging opens off Orchard Ground, which is locked at night, and only the Fellows of the College have keys…

'It is quite the most accomplished first crime novel that I have read…all first-rate entertainment'
– Cecil Day Lewis, *Daily Telegraph*

Michael Innes

Hamlet, Revenge!

At Seamnum Court, seat of the Duke of Horton, The Lord Chancellor of England is murdered at the climax of a private presentation of *Hamlet*, in which he plays Polonius. Inspector Appleby pursues some of the most famous names in the country, unearthing dreadful suspicion.

'Michael Innes is in a class by himself among writers of detective fiction' – *Times Literary Supplement*

The Long Farewell

Lewis Packford, the great Shakespearean scholar, was thought to have discovered a book annotated by the Bard – but there is no trace of this valuable object when Packford apparently commits suicide. Sir John Appleby finds a mixed bag of suspects at the dead man's house, who might all have a good motive for murder. The scholars and bibliophiles who were present might have been tempted by the precious document in Packford's possession. And Appleby discovers that Packford had two secret marriages, and that both of these women were at the house at the time of his death.

TITLES BY MICHAEL INNES AVAILABLE DIRECT
FROM HOUSE OF STRATUS

Quantity		£	$(US)	$(CAN)	€
	THE AMPERSAND PAPERS	6.99	12.95	19.95	13.50
	APPLEBY AND HONEYBATH	6.99	12.95	19.95	13.50
	APPLEBY AND THE OSPREYS	6.99	12.95	19.95	13.50
	APPLEBY AT ALLINGTON	6.99	12.95	19.95	13.50
	THE APPLEBY FILE	6.99	12.95	19.95	13.50
	APPLEBY ON ARARAT	6.99	12.95	19.95	13.50
	APPLEBY PLAYS CHICKEN	6.99	12.95	19.95	13.50
	APPLEBY TALKING	6.99	12.95	19.95	13.50
	APPLEBY TALKS AGAIN	6.99	12.95	19.95	13.50
	APPLEBY'S ANSWER	6.99	12.95	19.95	13.50
	APPLEBY'S END	6.99	12.95	19.95	13.50
	APPLEBY'S OTHER STORY	6.99	12.95	19.95	13.50
	AN AWKWARD LIE	6.99	12.95	19.95	13.50
	THE BLOODY WOOD	6.99	12.95	19.95	13.50
	A CHANGE OF HEIR	6.99	12.95	19.95	13.50
	CHRISTMAS AT CANDLESHOE	6.99	12.95	19.95	13.50
	A CONNOISSEUR'S CASE	6.99	12.95	19.95	13.50
	THE DAFFODIL AFFAIR	6.99	12.95	19.95	13.50
	DEATH AT THE CHASE	6.99	12.95	19.95	13.50
	DEATH AT THE PRESIDENT'S LODGING	6.99	12.95	19.95	13.50
	A FAMILY AFFAIR	6.99	12.95	19.95	13.50
	FROM LONDON FAR	6.99	12.95	19.95	13.50
	THE GAY PHOENIX	6.99	12.95	19.95	13.50
	GOING IT ALONE	6.99	12.95	19.95	13.50

ALL HOUSE OF STRATUS BOOKS ARE AVAILABLE FROM GOOD BOOKSHOPS OR
DIRECT FROM THE PUBLISHER:

Internet: www.houseofstratus.com including synopses and features.
Email: sales@houseofstratus.com
            info@houseofstratus.com
            (please quote author, title and credit card details.)

TITLES BY MICHAEL INNES AVAILABLE DIRECT
FROM HOUSE OF STRATUS

Quantity		£	$(US)	$(CAN)	€
	HAMLET, REVENGE!	6.99	12.95	19.95	13.50
	HARE SITTING UP	6.99	12.95	19.95	13.50
	HONEYBATH'S HAVEN	6.99	12.95	19.95	13.50
	THE JOURNEYING BOY	6.99	12.95	19.95	13.50
	LAMENT FOR A MAKER	6.99	12.95	19.95	13.50
	THE LONG FAREWELL	6.99	12.95	19.95	13.50
	LORD MULLION'S SECRET	6.99	12.95	19.95	13.50
	THE MAN FROM THE SEA	6.99	12.95	19.95	13.50
	MONEY FROM HOLME	6.99	12.95	19.95	13.50
	THE MYSTERIOUS COMMISSION	6.99	12.95	19.95	13.50
	THE NEW SONIA WAYWARD	6.99	12.95	19.95	13.50
	A NIGHT OF ERRORS	6.99	12.95	19.95	13.50
	OLD HALL, NEW HALL	6.99	12.95	19.95	13.50
	THE OPEN HOUSE	6.99	12.95	19.95	13.50
	OPERATION PAX	6.99	12.95	19.95	13.50
	A PRIVATE VIEW	6.99	12.95	19.95	13.50
	THE SECRET VANGUARD	6.99	12.95	19.95	13.50
	SHEIKS AND ADDERS	6.99	12.95	19.95	13.50
	SILENCE OBSERVED	6.99	12.95	19.95	13.50
	STOP PRESS	6.99	12.95	19.95	13.50
	THERE CAME BOTH MIST AND SNOW	6.99	12.95	19.95	13.50
	THE WEIGHT OF THE EVIDENCE	6.99	12.95	19.95	13.50
	WHAT HAPPENED AT HAZELWOOD	6.99	12.95	19.95	13.50

ALL HOUSE OF STRATUS BOOKS ARE AVAILABLE FROM GOOD BOOKSHOPS OR
DIRECT FROM THE PUBLISHER:

Tel: Order Line
          0800 169 1780 (UK)
           800 724 1100 (USA)
          International
          +44 (0) 1845 527700 (UK)
          +01   845 463 1100 (USA)

Fax: +44 (0) 1845 527711 (UK)
          +01   845 463 0018 (USA)
          (please quote author, title and credit card details.)

Send to: House of Stratus Sales Department   House of Stratus Inc.
          Thirsk Industrial Park   2 Neptune Road
          York Road, Thirsk   Poughkeepsie
          North Yorkshire, YO7 3BX   NY 12601
          UK   USA

PAYMENT

Please tick currency you wish to use:

☐ £ (Sterling)   ☐ $ (US)   ☐ $ (CAN)   ☐ € (Euros)

Allow for shipping costs charged per order plus an amount per book as set out in the tables below:

CURRENCY/DESTINATION

	£(Sterling)	$(US)	$(CAN)	€ (Euros)
Cost per order				
UK	1.50	2.25	3.50	2.50
Europe	3.00	4.50	6.75	5.00
North America	3.00	3.50	5.25	5.00
Rest of World	3.00	4.50	6.75	5.00
Additional cost per book				
UK	0.50	0.75	1.15	0.85
Europe	1.00	1.50	2.25	1.70
North America	1.00	1.00	1.50	1.70
Rest of World	1.50	2.25	3.50	3.00

PLEASE SEND CHEQUE OR INTERNATIONAL MONEY ORDER
payable to: HOUSE OF STRATUS LTD or HOUSE OF STRATUS INC. or card payment as indicated

STERLING EXAMPLE

Cost of book(s):..................... Example: 3 x books at £6.99 each: £20.97
Cost of order: .... Example: £1.50 (Delivery to UK address)
Additional cost per book:.............. Example: 3 x £0.50: £1.50
Order total including shipping:........... Example: £23.97

VISA, MASTERCARD, SWITCH, AMEX:

☐ ☐ ☐ ☐ ☐ ☐ ☐ ☐ ☐ ☐ ☐ ☐ ☐ ☐ ☐ ☐ ☐ ☐ ☐ ☐

Issue number (Switch only):

☐ ☐ ☐

Start Date: **Expiry Date:**

☐ ☐ / ☐ ☐   ☐ ☐ / ☐ ☐

Signature: _____

NAME: _____

ADDRESS: _____

COUNTRY: _____

ZIP/POSTCODE: _____

Please allow 28 days for delivery. Despatch normally within 48 hours.

Prices subject to change without notice.
Please tick box if you do not wish to receive any additional information. ☐

House of Stratus publishes many other titles in this genre; please check our
website (**www.houseofstratus.com**) for more details.